A
Broken
Man

By the same author

It Happened That Night

Three Times Loser

A
Broken
Man

AKASH VERMA

Srishti
PUBLISHERS & DISTRIBUTORS

SRISHTI PUBLISHERS & DISTRIBUTORS
Registered Office: N-16, C.R. Park
New Delhi – 110 019
Corporate Office: 212A, Peacock Lane
Shahpur Jat, New Delhi – 110 049
editorial@srishtipublishers.com

First published by
Srishti Publishers & Distributors in 2016

As long as one has hope, there is nothing one cannot achieve; everything is born from hope.
— Daisaku Ikeda

Daisaku Ikeda is a Buddhist philosopher, peace builder, educator, author and poet. He is the third president of the Soka Gakkai and the founding president of the Soka Gakkai International (SGI).

Acknowledgements

Thank You.

To the cities of Lucknow and Mumbai: the warmth of their memories oozes into my stories.

The villages of Bihar: I was fortunate to be in your company for the first time as I developed *A Broken Man*. You are truly beautiful, simple, and giving.

To my parents: I owe my writing to you.

My family and friends: your support as always has been incredible.

Srishti Publishers: for believing in my stories and making them read better.

Finally, all the Chhavis in this world. Thank you, for shaping the lives of more and more Krishnas.

Mumbai: 31st December, 2015

The black Mercedes Benz rolled up to face the palatial entry gates of the swanky Malibu Towers in Bandra West, Mumbai. The CCTV camera perched on one of the walls craned its head to acknowledge that the car belonged to this high end condominium – sea-facing, five thousand square feet apartments that overlooked the majestic Arabian Sea. The automated gates opened swiftly to let the car enter this haven of splendour that seemed to be cut off from the rest of humanity. It was New Year's Eve, yet the condominium was soaked in an eerie calm; in complete contrast with the celebrations that marked the city outside the boundary of Malibu Towers.

Ram Singh Yadav looked upwards at the dimly-lit vast balconies that rested in front of each apartment. A few of them had decked themselves up with a minimalistic array of lights, to make them look chic and occasion-friendly, yet subtle enough to stay away from being labelled as distracting and loud. Even the balconies of Malibu Towers looked conscious of their lineage, forget the people who lived there. They came from all walks of life – investment bankers, company CEOs, film stars, industrialists, politicians – having that one thing in common, a non-satiating lust for money.

Ram Singh Yadav pulled up the luxury sedan in front of the C Block and glanced at the rear view mirror. KK, his employer and 'sahib' for the last twelve years gulped the last sip of vodka from the glass and placed it back in the holder, nestled in the arm-rest of the car's back seat.

The two men sat motionless for a few moments – one looking at the other through the rear view mirror, the other staring at the dark oblivion outside. Ram Singh murmured, 'Sir, we have reached home.'

KK moved his gaze to the mirror where his eyes met his driver's. He nodded his head gently and pushed open the car door. KK got out of the car and straightened his body that was engulfed with a strange sense of serene that emanated after three large shots of Grey Goose Vodka, coupled with bodily weariness that was the result of a two-hour drive from South Mumbai, after a daylong gruelling story discussion with Crescent Studios.

KK walked towards the entrance briskly, leaving the car and the driver behind. Ram Singh lifted himself out of the car to pick up the empty glass and the half-filled vodka bottle. He pushed a tiny trunk release button on the car key to open it. The trunk opened up with a twitch to expose the vast space that the sedan carried within. He wiped the glass with a tissue and kept it in a box placed on one side of the boot and slipped the bottle carefully into a customized decanter.

It had been twelve long years that he had been with KK, one of the most sought after and successful scriptwriters and lyricists of Hindi film industry, and perhaps his only friend in this big city that considered people like him outsiders.

Ram Singh had landed in Mumbai after a catastrophe had struck his native village in Bihar. Incessant rainfall and floods had robbed millions of their land, housing, and eventually an opportunity to live. For Ram Singh, the scars were harsher and much deeper. He had lost his wife and two little children to the water that devoured them as he cried hoarsely, clinging atop his mud thatched roof. The water was everywhere: on the ground, in the air, on his body and fiercely pouring through his eyes. He could never forget what he last saw of his family as they unsuccessfully tried to defeat the mammoth force of the ravaging stream. The sleeve of his younger son's red-coloured check shirt, that he had got stitched for a cousin's wedding the previous year, and the pain in his wife's eyes as she looked at him for the last time before getting pulled down by the gushing water. Was it the fear of death, the pang of separation or the helplessness of being the chosen one to die so wastefully? The memory haunted Ram Singh every day, endlessly, groping him for an answer which never came. After languishing in grief for a year, Ram Singh decided to take control of his life again. He came to Mumbai with a sad heart and an empty stomach, hoping to start afresh, leaving his pitiful story behind in his native village, in that ravaging flood, in those pain-filled eyes of his wife.

Ram Singh Yadav landed in Mumbai with meagre cash and a few addresses of his relatives who could perhaps help him find a source of living in the chaos of the city. Mumbai was well-known to accomplish a million dreams, yet cruel enough to break a billion hearts. The only thing that Ram Singh knew besides growing crops was driving. Back in his village, he was the proud owner of a tractor that he drove across his fields with aplomb. During weekdays, when not taking it to the field, he would drive it to the neighbouring town for household purchases, or to buy seeds and fertilizers. At the time of celebratory occasions like marriage, the tractor would ferry family and friends from one village to another.

Ram Singh enrolled himself with a local driving school in Mahim. As he held the steering wheel of the car, he was reminded of his tractor rolling on the bumpy village roads with his family resting happily at the back. It was strange, yet cathartic; the more he drove, the happier he felt.

Ram Singh Yadav first met KK at RK studios in Chembur, while he had gone there to meet his relative who drove for a film producer. After catching up on pleasantries and Raghu handing him a half-an-hour dose on the cruelty of fate and never-changing harsh karma, Ram Singh asked him for a job reference.

'You have come here at the right time, Ram Singh. It's all in destiny and the stars,' Raghu said. By now it was evident to Ram Singh that Raghu was into the habit of interpreting everything to be a working of destiny, stars, and karma. Perhaps his morning dump as well.

'There is a guy working with Malhotra Sahib on his new film. I don't know his name, but everyone calls him KK,' Raghu said puffing away from the cigarette.

"KK, what kind of a name is that? What does he do? Anyway, can you make me meet him, Raghu?' Ram Singh asked.

'He is a good man, Ram Singh. KK sahib writes stories and songs,' Raghu said.

"He writes a story and a song? But what does he do for a living?' Ram Singh asked confused.

KK was unlocking his Maruti 800 in the evening when someone called him from behind.

'Sahib, I want you to meet Ram Singh. He is from our village in Bihar and has come here looking for a job. That day you had mentioned to Malhotra sir's assistant that you wanted a driver. KK sahib, I had overheard. You can trust him,' Raghu said in a sweetened voice.

Two things about KK had stuck Ram Singh when he saw him for the first time. First, his magnetic personality, for he seemed to exude a positive energy that had a calming influence all around. There wasn't any man like KK that he had seen before, neither in his native village nor anywhere else. Second, Ram Singh thought, KK had eyes that ached of pain. Ram Singh Yadav had stopped looking at himself in the mirror, but whenever accidentally he found himself looking into one, his eyes looked out of place. When he saw KK, his eyes found a partner.

KK took a waited look at the dark, thinly-built moustached man who was balding faster than his progressing age. His dark skin was perhaps a result of spending numerous hours under the scorching sun in the village fields, and the wrinkles that had sprung up so early on his face were possibly due to an uncalled for suffering early in life. KK was not a man unknown to such a life.

'Where have you worked earlier in Mumbai, Ram Singh?' KK asked calmly.

'Sir, just finished my training at the motor learning school. This is my first job interview,' Ram Singh said hesitatingly.

'Hmm...Have you driven earlier in Mumbai? I mean, it would take a lot of time for you to be comfortable on these chaotic Mumbai roads,' KK said.

'Sahib, if I could meander my tractor through the morasses in the fields, the bumpy single lane of my village with my entire family safe throughout the journey, the roads here will never be an issue,' Ram Singh replied .

KK patted his shoulder, 'Ok, Ram Singh, come from tomorrow. Raghu, please give him the directions to my house,' KK gestured to Raghu and drove off.

KK had, since that moment, always treated Ram Singh as an equal, a friend, and his family, for he had none in that city. Ram Singh Yadav was forever indebted to KK from that day, for he had held his hand when both destiny and God had deserted him.

Ram Singh shut the large boot with a gentle push and followed KK towards the elevators. KK swiped the door card to enter his lavish apartment. The automated light sensors started working as he walked a few steps through the lit alley into the giant living room. The lighting was dim, as KK didn't like bright lights that brought out the lavish splendour of the apartment. He thought it was an absolutely grotesque manner to display one's wealth. The thought of leaving his modest two bedroom apartment in Bandra would have never crossed KK's mind, if not for producer Vinod Khanna.

'KK, my friend, it won't work like this anymore. You are now amongst the top writers from Bollywood and living here doesn't suit you image,' Vinod Khanna had glanced around his apartment in Versova as he kept the scotch-filled glass on the table.

'But why Khanna ji? Do people like me for what I write or for where I live!' KK had replied.

'Don't be unnecessarily stubborn, KK. There is a reason why I have been coaxing you for over six months now.

In this industry, you need to call people over, all kinds of people, from producers and directors to the media. You just can't keep meeting them in coffee shops, for heaven's sake,' Vinod Khanna had this habit of rushing through his words when excited.

'You know what I feel about the house thing, Khanna ji. You pushing me so hard for it...doesn't make your argument stronger,' KK replied nonchalantly.

'That's why no more pleas,' Khanna said and took out a bunch of keys from his jacket pocket.

'What's that Khanna ji?' His alacrity had alarmed KK.

'C-705, Malibu Towers – your home from today,' Khanna announced like a true blue producer launching a new film in front of the media.

'Those seven star residential apartments?' KK was shocked. 'I don't have that kind of money.'

'Do you ask for money when you write my films?' Khanna asked. 'Don't dress up our relationship with something as inexpensive as money,' Khanna said emotionally.

The next day, KK moved into the luxury of Malibu Towers and it became his new abode.

KK pressed a switch on the main panel. The curtains covering the giant living room windows opened up to display the beauty of the Arabian Sea. This was the part he liked most about this apartment, the view. Religiously, every day after entering the apartment, this was the first thing KK would do. Like a ritual he would soak himself into the calmness of the night that embraced the beauty of the mammoth sea. Those were his moments of freedom, from the tribulations of the above average work that he was forced to churn out most of the days and the pain that his heart had carried for so many years.

It was that night of the year for which he had waited for all those other three hundred and sixty-four days, every year, for the last so many years. December 31ˢᵗ. KK had never celebrated his birthday that fell on the New Year's Day, despite repeated requests from friends belonging to the industry. He would politely turn them down, year after another. Like every other New Year's Eve, he waited for his only cherished birthday present.

Chhavi would write to him that day to wish him. Just one line: Happy Birthday Krishna. There was nothing more that KK would long for in the entire year than reading this one line, every year. That one line from her was like a slender thread, which connected him back to the maze of memories that he had left behind. The memories deeply buried, yet alive, reminiscent of Chhavi and Krishna.

'Sir, the keys are on the table,' Ram Singh interrupted his thoughts.

'Ok, Ram Singh. I will see you tomorrow,' KK muttered and Ram Singh left the apartment.

KK poured himself another drink from the well-stuffed bar and put the laptop on the bar counter. He tapped on his mail Inbox; there were a few spam e-mails, wishes from friends on the eastern side of the world for whom the New Year had already arrived, and work-related mails from his assistant script-writers. None was from her as yet. He looked at his watch; it was 11.30, still some time for his birthday to arrive. He opened his personal folder on the MacBook, and clicked on the sub-folder titled "Chhavi" within it. It was further coded into sixteen more folders that were titled by the years in numerals – 2000, 2001...till they reached 2015. KK clicked on "New Folder", named it 2016 and watched it sit gently beneath the rest of the sixteen. He tapped the cursor on the folder titled 2000, 'Happy Birthday Krishna,' the message read. He tapped on the next one; it too had the same message. He kept reading them all till he reached folder 2015; the message was the same.

Celebrations began with the burst of crackers all around the Malibu Towers that broke KK's stupor at midnight. He got up and walked to his balcony. The fireworks had lit up the sky to underline the darkened veil of the winter night and disturb the tranquillity of the waters that lay ahead. KK switched on the TV and rested himself on the bar stool again. Sony channel was showing a recent Bollywood blockbuster; he had written the story for it. He quickly changed the channel to one that showed Hollywood movies, where they were showing *Titanic*. He was really fond of the film's screenplay despite watching it many times before. The story of Jack Dawson and Rose. He had always been fascinated with love stories that never end.

The unseen anxiety in his heart woke him up with a jolt. He looked at the watch and rushed to his MacBook; it was 5.30 a.m. He refreshed his e-mail folder repeatedly, but it didn't show any new e-mail. He checked the entire day's e-mails once again, hoping that he would have perhaps missed something, but he hadn't. He sat motionless in front of the computer screen for a few moments, assimilating conflicting thoughts and emotions that danced like streaks of fire in his mind. He took a deep breath and went to his preferred online travel portal. As he typed the alphabet L on the destination field, the portal picked up "LUCKNOW". He clicked on it to find that none of the flights from any airline were available to fly to Lucknow on that day.

'Good morning. Quick Go airlines. How can I help you?' the telecaller sounded pretty alert even at such an early hour.

'Why aren't there any flights to Lucknow?' KK rushed.

'Sir, dense fog in North India, we aren't taking a chance to fly anywhere else other that Delhi,' she replied.

'No possibility of a flight today or tomorrow?" KK asked.

'It doesn't seem possible today sir; tomorrow's situation would only be clear by the afternoon today. Anything else I can do for you sir?'

KK ended the call. He reached out to the train booking section on the portal, which showed non availability of tickets on any superfast trains. He knew the winter law that worked during these extreme months in northern India – endless cancellations and delays of flights along with a 24-to-48 hour late arrival of trains, due to intense weather conditions. Nature can just beat the shit out of any amount of manmade controls that you would want to rout it with. The wait for the afternoon was impossible for KK to deal with. In fact, with every passing moment, the uneasiness was growing within, multiplying. He had to find out the reason behind her not writing to him today. Even if it meant breaking the promise that he had made to her on that cold night at the forlorn railway platform years back. He had to reach out to her again.

'Sir, so early in the morning? Is everything fine?' Ram Singh was cooking his lunch when KK called.

'Ram Singh, can you come as soon as possible? And yes, don't forget to keep some clothes; we might be gone for a few days,' KK spoke as he packed his suitcase.

'Ok sahib, I will reach in less than an hour. But where are we going?' he asked looking out of the window of his 1BHK apartment that KK had rented for him in Vile Parle East.

'Lucknow,' KK said after a moment of silence.

'Sir, why are we going to Lucknow? Another story that you want to write?' Ram Singh was perplexed after driving the car in complete silence for over two hours. KK had never behaved like this before. Anxious, deep in thought, it was as if he was in some other land, where his mind and his body operated at two different levels.

'No, Ram Singh, this story has been written years ago,' KK replied, resting his head on the front seat of the luxury sedan that raced through the heart of National Highway No. 3.

'I want to listen to it KK Sahib. I really want to hear your story,' Ram Singh spoke earnestly with his eyes on the wide gaping highway.

KK heaved a deep sigh and said, 'My name is Krishna, Ram Singh. I want you to hear my story.' His over-burdened heart threw up to reveal what it had been holding for years.

Lucknow University: June, 1999

The afternoon sun eyed vengeance on the city inhabitants by unleashing its full potential. Chhavi stood under the legendary banyan tree of the Arts Canteen, perspiring, yet holding the mike and her demeanour, severely tested by the weather. The motley crowd that squeezed itself under the shade to listen to her was not helping; it added on to the suffocation.

'What a year it has been for the country and this university! The same issues that are pulling this country down are hell bent on grazing this wonderful citadel of education. Am I right?' she raised her pitch.

The crowd marooned under the sweltering heat looked disinterested in cracking political riddles. They cared more about dissecting a good looking girl from such close quarters. It was an uncommon sight in north India, where students coming from god forsaken villages of Uttar Pradesh and Bihar could actually get to look at a fair girl dressed fashionably. Also, that she was standing at an arm's length from them.

'In Delhi, we fight against reservation and corruption, yet the same issues plague our University here. I am surprised that all of you here, including me, face this every single day.' She smiled sarcastically.

'She smiles like Madhuri,' a besotted guy from Bihar exclaimed to his friend. Madhuri Dixit was then the Bollywood heartthrob of every male that walked the landscape of India.

'There are eighteen students in arts, seven in science at the graduation level and fourteen more at the post-graduation level who have sneaked into this university under the quota system. There is a nexus between the leaders that you have appointed and corrupt university officials,' her voice stamped the mike.

The look of indifference mellowed and murmurs erupted in the group. Reservation was a burning issue of the times that impacted the future of the students directly. The country was alive with widespread agitations, both peaceful and violent, amongst the student fraternity. Mandal that had surfaced in 1990 was still alive.

'Who are these students? We want to know the names,' one of the listeners shouted excitedly.

'Yes, we won't tolerate this disorder here. Give us the names,' another *khadi*-clad bespectacled student raised his voice.

'I have the names here, but I won't give them to you,' Chhavi said waving a piece of paper in front of the crowd.

'Because these students are not to be blamed so much; they are gullible like me and you here. Those who push them to walk the path laden with deceit are the real culprits. They are the ones who need to be taken to task and be exposed,' she said.

'Who are they anyway? We want to know,' more voices erupted.

'You will be surprised, very surprised like me,' Chhavi spoke theatrically, addressing a crowd that looked seemingly charmed.

'These thirty-nine students, all of them, incidentally belong to the two districts from where your revered and favourite leaders hail. Gajaraj Singh Gope and Akhil Tiwari.'

The faces in the crowd displayed brazen disbelief, disgust, and anger.

'It can be a coincidence, but such a bizarre one seems unlikely,' she rounded up her statement.

'Can you prove that this has been engineered at the behest of Gope and Akhil Tiwari?' a student protested.

'That's the job of the authorities and the law, not ours. I, along with my party comrades, have unearthed some facts in front of you today. Now it's for you decide; ask your leaders who stand vindicated in front of this naked truth. It's time we ask them some tough questions,' Chhavi said weighing each word.

'Our party might be young, it may be small as compared to the large forces that we are fighting against, but one thing is certain – we are not afraid to speak and neither are we to fight. Our job is to ensure safeguarding students' rights and this university's dignity, and to uphold the truth. We call ourselves CSWI – the Common Student Wing of India – because we represent students, our most cherished treasure.' Chhavi smiled warmly, opening her arms to hint at the crowd.

'Jai Hind. Jai Lucknow University!' She raised the slogan excitedly on the microphone thrice with the CSWI comrades joining her chant in unison.

'It went off quite well, Chhavi. Good work,' Ravi, her colleague from the party, muttered in her ears as the other members of CSWI busied themselves in distributing party pamphlets amongst the crowd that had started dispersing. A few still remained glued to their places feasting their eyes one last time on the pretty damsel who could speak so well.

'I hope so Ravi, but we have a lot of ground to cover in a very short time or we would let guys like Gope and Tiwari rule over this University.' She wiped off the sweat on the forehead with her white dupatta.

'Yes, with six months left for the election, we have our task clearly cut out. Many such meetings should happen from now till the University goes for polls. No?' Ravi said.

Chhavi nodded and patted his shoulder. 'Lesser time will motivate us to work harder and will make it tougher for our opponents to realize what we are up to. By the time they realize our game plan, hopefully their game would be over. You need to look at the brighter side of this situation, Ravi.'

A small group that had been a part of the crowd that was listening to Chhavi gathered around the steps of the Arts College Canteen, sipping tea.

'Abhay bhaiya, the girl surely has some guts, speaking like that up here,' Bittu's tone was full of admiration.

'If you are so impressed, why don't you go and join her insignificant party!' Abhay rebuked him paying scant attention to Bittu's admiration. Bittu's face fell and he instantly shut his mouth.

'Do you know who this girl is?' Abhay said taking a sip. The group went silent.

'Panditji's daughter, Chhavi Shankar Mishra, B.Sc Second Year Geology,' one of the students from the group replied. The silence within the group evaporated and they looked flustered like hell.

'What is she doing here? I mean with this petty party like CSWI? Never heard about her before,' Bittu said raising his arms animatedly.

'Bittu, you speak as if you have the whereabouts of all the students studying here. Bloody, you wouldn't even know the room where your classes are held, or let's bet, you would not even know what your subjects are. Come on, can you tell me?' Abhay chided him.

'Umm...History...I think Political Science...Abhay bhaiya,' Bittu stammered as students around him chuckled. Abhay shook his head with repulsion and then his face hardened.

'This is not good. If she has more of such interactions with the students, there will be too many questions that will become tough for us to answer. Gope bhaiya should know about this,' Abhay said and kept the cup down.

The Tilak Hostel in the backyard of the Lucknow University was warming up for an unpleasant evening after an exceedingly hot day. Abhay and Bittu walked briskly towards Room No. 14, which fell in the left wing of the hostel and faced the open courtyard of about a hundred-year-old hostel building. They negotiated their way through the randomly parked two-wheelers and cycles of the students to face the room of Gajaraj Singh Gope on the ground floor of the building. Gope was the current president of the University students union and was running for the same post, the second time. He had been walking the corridors of Lucknow University for close to ten years now and had no plans to leave it soon enough, for which place would automatically catapult you, onto the spiralling expanse of state politics of Uttar Pradesh, a haven where you could dig out as much power and wealth as you wanted. Gope, who had been increasing his vote and support base through thumping victory in the University elections, was the right fodder that the parties in reckoning looked out for. He drew his support from Bhartiya Samaj Party (BSP) that ruled the state currently, but was still growing its stature nationally by clinging on to the Hindu identity that it wanted to evoke amongst the majority Hindu population within the country. BSP was the national opposition for Lok Shakti Party (LSP) that was almost a hundred years old in the country, the leaders from which had ushered in the Indian Independence. Lok Shakti was a centrally controlled machine run by a particular dynasty for a long time; it was currently in opposition in the state. It was covertly supporting Akhil Tiwari, another formidable student leader in the University who was pitted against Gope in the coming elections for the post of the President.

The door of Gope's room was partially shut and two hearty students guarded it like sentinels. Abhay and Bittu entered the door without hesitation and brought the discussion happening inside to a halt. Gope was an exact replica of a burly dacoit from one of those true blood Hindi bandit movies – a puffed-up charcoal coloured dark face, small suspicion-laden eyes, overweight body that could not hold any clothes except loosely fitted white kurta and pyjama, and a gruff voice that spelt danger.

Gope turned his face away from the group that sat around him, and smiled at Abhay reluctantly. 'So how was the university today, Abhay? Come sit,' he gestured at the mattress sprawled in front of the cushioned wooden bed that he sat on.

Abhay planted his bottom on the mattress and spoke in a measured tone, 'What happened today doesn't augur well for us.' Gope raised his eyebrows and gestured at him to speak further. He heard the story with an expressionless face and spoke after a few minutes of silence.

'Panditji's daughter is trying to spark a revolution in the university? Well, this sounds interesting,' he said thoughtfully.

'What should we do bhaiya? Disrupt her meetings? For this can't go on,' Abhay muttered.

Gope raised his hand to interrupt him, 'No, not with Panditji's daughter. He is one of the senior-most leaders of Lok Shakti in the state. Anything we do against his daughter would seem like an act of BSP routed through us; high command would not be happy.'

'Then what do we do bhaiya? Sit here like eunuchs as she keeps wrapping us like idiots, the way she did today?' Abhay said hastily .

'Shhh...,' Gope said with his finger on the lip. 'Don't be stupid! I just said we will not do it. We, meaning all of you, who the world knows as my associates.'

'We need to find someone amongst us, someone who has a point to prove, to me and to the world outside. Someone whose face the world doesn't associate with ours.' Gope succumbed into his thoughts shutting his eyes.

He opened them after a while. 'Call Krishna to meet me in the morning tomorrow. Abhay, will you do that for me?'

Abhay raised his eyebrows. 'Do I hear you correctly? That Dalit from Subhash Hostel... Krishna?' he confirmed in an unpleasant tone. Gope looked at him and nodded resolutely.

The cycle rickshaw navigated a sharp turn to enter the lane that housed the grandest bungalows of Nirala Nagar, B Block.

Chhavi Shankar Mishra asked the rickshaw puller to stop to get down in front of her white-coloured, three-floored bungalow that hosted a huge garden, large enough to accommodate a dozen normal houses. A stream of vehicles were lined outside the bungalow, a few belonging to the fleet that her father Pandit Radhey Shankar Mishra and her two brothers possessed, while the others to the overflowing stream of visitors that filled the lane whenever the senior politician was in town. Radhey Shankar Mishra, fondly called Panditji by everyone, was a veteran politician who took an active part in the state politics for over forty years. An associate of the Lok Shakti Party right from the onset, he grew from the lower rungs to become one of the central faces of the state leadership. All owing to his hard work, courage and the tenacity with which he went about to get something done. *Panditji can't break or bend, if he has set out to achieve something* – was the adage that followed him.

Chhavi walked through the gate on the pathway that led her to the bungalow, under the shade of trees that stood tall on both sides, interrupted frequently by a few guards who carried arms hanging loosely over their shoulder while a few who stood with holsters carrying pistols. She had grown up with these perks that came along with being the daughter of one of the most influential politicians in Uttar Pradesh. The men nodded gently to show respect as she walked through them and entered the house. She could hear her father's voice amidst others, deeply engrossed in discussion, and decided to enter the house through the other door. It was locked, so she knocked on the door.

'Who is it?' His deep baritone filled the lobby.

'It's me Baba,' she replied.

'Chhavi, is that you. Why don't you come here to show me your face? It's been so many days,' her father's voice smoothened.

She entered the living room tentatively, not knowing who the visitors could be. Panditji sat in the centre wearing his traditional white kurta and pyjama. He was a man with kind eyes and a warm smile. He got up from the cushioned sofa to hug her and then he stroked her head.

'Where do you come from, it's been so hot today?' He looked concerned.

'I was at the University, Baba. It is bearable, not that bad,' she replied looking around with a warm smile, acknowledging others in the room.

'She has grown up swiftly into a fine young lady,' one of them said as Chhavi tried to figure out who that gentleman was.

'Don't you recognize him Chhavi? The current MP Pandeyji from Lakhimpur. We met him last at his nephew's wedding at Clarks, about two years back, no?' he looked at the short-statured, gentle looking Pandeyji standing next to him.

Chhavi could remember going to this particular wedding, but couldn't remember him at all. Anyway, all of them looked similar wearing the same white-coloured kurta pyjama. She sheepishly shook her head as they laughed gently.

Panditji spoke sombrely, 'When her mother passed away twenty years back, she was about a year old. Anil was also just about three and Vijay, seven. I have been so busy in politics since then, that I have had no time to look after their upbringing. If it was not for their grandmother, I wouldn't have been able to walk this far.'

'There is a reason why everything happens the way it happens. It is only later that we get to realize the motive behind it,' Pandeyji, the MP, added thoughtfully.

'Baba, please excuse me, I have some task to attend to.'

'Sure, my child! Let's talk more over dinner tonight. Please ask your brothers to eat at home for the next two-three days. I am going to be here in the city. We hardly get time together as a family,' saying this, her father made way for her to exit the room.

Chhavi was climbing the stairs to her room on the first floor when she met her grandmother walking down. 'Nani, I am famished. Can I get something to eat please?' she pleaded.

'Where have you been the whole day, Chhavi? Go wash your hands and face and come down to the kitchen. I am frying pakoras for snacks,' Nani's words made her mouth water.

'I was out Nani, on a date,' Chhavi mocked.

'What??' Her old grandmother freaked out. The only time a woman went out alone with a guy in their family was after exchanging holy vows.

'Relax, Nani! Before you collapse… I was in the University, darling!' she pulled her Nani's withered cheeks gently. 'Will be downstairs in a minute.'

'So what's the news on upcoming LU (Lucknow University) elections Panditji? They are not too far,' Pandeyji said after having settled on the sofa again. The University elections were a contest like Ranji trophy in cricket; a good performance there meant you had a chance to get into the national team.

'Akhil Tiwari has visited me twice to seek my blessings and advice, but he is very aggressive and doesn't think from here,' Panditji pointed towards his forehead. 'The sentiment for our party is strong, but BSP is also trying to cash on this Mandal issue. You know, trying to garner all high caste votes by taking a strong stance against reservation. We are trying to balance it,' Panditji said, thinking.

'Yes, why not! Balance power and intellect, balance upper and lower caste, create equilibrium, the Lok Shakti way of politics,' Pandeyji smiled to himself.

'Why not Pandeyji, not just our mother earth but the entire universe exists on this delicate equilibrium. It is the single most crucial thing that maintains balance between nature, plants, animals, and human beings. The founder members of Lok Shakti were smart enough to realize this – No point in taking a radical stance,' Panditji paused. 'Just take the middle path; no need to wander to the extreme left or right.'

'Krishna! O Krishna!' Abhay's voice reverberated through the spacious corridors of Subhash Hostel early in the morning. A few students who had been up early to study were jolted by the sudden loud voice bursting into their rooms. Some others walking towards the common bathroom looked down from the first floor, with foam-filled mouths, and surprised puffy eyes.

The morning sun was growing sharper by the minute. Abhay looked up once again and shouted, this time raising his pitch. The wooden door of the room creaked and the hinges murmured loudly in protest as Krishna came out in the balcony, wearing a banyan over a crumpled pyjama. He looked startled with this early morning intrusion; it reflected clearly on his bronzed face as he looked at Abhay.

'Abhay bhaiya, what brings you here so early today?' he exclaimed.

'What does Gope see in this low caste nerd, who neither has the pedigree nor the intelligence to be a part of us,' he muttered to the boy standing next to him. Then, looked up and shouted out loud. 'Gope wants to meet you as soon as possible. How soon can you come?'

'Gope bhaiya is calling me?' Krishna said gratefully, 'I will be there in half an hour.'

'Ok. Don't be late,' Abhay said and walked away. Krishna raised both his arms to stretch his naturally muscular and tall body, a result of years of hard-work that it had undergone at his native village in Bihar. He yawned once and entered his room to get ready.

Krishna knocked softly on the door of Gope's room in Tilak Hostel. It couldn't be heard by the people inside as they spoke amongst themselves at higher decibels. He knocked firmly one more time.

'Who's there? Come inside,' Gope spoke loudly.

Krishna entered the room where Gope was perched on the wooden cot surrounded by six burly students who looked more like goons. They were engrossed in an animated conversation and none of them looked pleased to see Krishna, except Gope.

'How are you Krishna? Haven't seen you for a while. Come, sit!' Gope gestured at the floor.

'I had been preparing for the exams, bhaiya,' Krishna said, his dialect still reeked heavily of his native village in Bihar. Four years in Lucknow, yet Bihar wasn't left behind; he still carried it in his speech and mannerisms.

'What will you do with so much studying? Want to become a collector?' Abhay sniggered.

'Why can't he become one? Reservation is turning low caste morons into collectors, doctors, engineers, government babus and what not,' Bittu sitting next to him said stingingly.

Krishna clenched his teeth and kept his gaze glued to the floor.

'Just shut up, Bittu! I have called Krishna to discuss something important,' Gope reprimanded him, shutting up all others in the process. 'Want some water, Krishna? It's very hot outside; drink some water and then we will talk. Bittu, why don't you get some cold water for him?'

Bittu got up rather reluctantly and picked up a Bisleri bottle from the table and stood in front of Krishna who squatted on the cemented floor. Krishna cupped both his hands as Bittu poured water in it.

'So, why did you call for me Gope bhaiya?' Krishna felt better after drinking water.

'Have you heard Panditji's name, Krishna?' Gope asked.

Krishna nodded in affirmation.

'So what do you want me to do?' Krishna asked after hearing Gope's abridged version of Panditji's daughter trying to sabotage his reputation. More than the image he seemed to be more concerned about someone trying to get in the way of his second stint as the University president. He didn't seem to be in a mood to take any chance.

'Disrupt her meetings. Make sure that they end midway. Create confusion among the crowd that gathers to listen to her. Start by using words, but if that doesn't work, use force,' Gope said coldly.

'But why have you chosen me, bhaiya?' Krishna asked, glancing at the army surrounding Gope.

'Hmm...,' Gope paused. 'Well, no one knows you Krishna. You are an obscure name and one face amongst the thousands who fill this university. Everybody here knows them and our association. I don't want my name to come into this at all,' he said aiming his finger at the cluster, some seated on the cot, others standing.

'You had requested me once that you wanted to be an active part of student politics. No?' Gope asked. Krishna nodded.

'So, all of this is part and parcel of this animal called politics. It gives you name, recognition, power, money, and what not. But you have to dirty your hands a bit.' Gope smiled at him condescendingly.

'Will you do this and prove your solidarity to me, Krishna?'

'I will, bhaiya,' Krishna replied looking into his eyes.

There was silence in the room for a few minutes after Krishna walked out.

'Gope bhaiya, why let this chamar handle such a crucial thing? What if something goes wrong?' Abhay asked crisply.

Gope smiled meaningfully. 'Nothing will go amiss Abhay, and even if it does, a chamar would be disrupting the meeting of a high caste Mishra girl; everyone would blame it on his frustration and resentment against her caste. No one would be able to trace our involvement in this.'

Abhay clasped his palms together and bowed down before Gope. 'You truly are a master politician bhaiya.' The room resonated with loud guffaws henceforth.

'Why did you agree to Gope?' Shiv asked as he sat on the chair in the hostel room. He was Krishna's room-mate and another low-caste from Jagdishpur village a couple of kilometres away from his.

'What's the option before us, Shiv? I don't want to live an inconsequential unknown life anymore. Haven't we lived like this enough?' Krishna lay flat on the bed, facing the ceiling.

'This hooliganism isn't going to give you that life Krishna. We are here to study and earn a living. Do better than the people we have left behind in our villages,' Shiv argued.

'You call this rowdiness; I call it disruption. It is only when you disrupt the natural that you get noticed in this world.'

'They are not going to give us a gold medal and a government job for doing this,' Shiv said.

Krishna looked at Shiv. 'What will you do with a reservation-granted, small government job, Shiv? Scrape a few inches ahead than your father and forefathers. Have a pucca house in place of the one with mud walls and a thatched roof, live in Patna as against Jagdishpur, make fifteen thousand bucks a month rather than the three that your father makes currently working his ass off all day?'

'Isn't that better than what we have been used to?' Shiv asked.

'Making our life better than the one we currently have... Is that all your dreams are about?' Krishna asked.

'Our reality is a bitter pill that prohibits dreams,' Shiv said.

Krishna moved his gaze to the ceiling again. 'Well it's just the opposite with me. My dreams are like a fire burning inside my heart.'

Shiv smiled. 'Bloody chamar ke. You have problems in speaking correct Hindi, forget English, and you want to take on the high caste world.'

'Who said battles are won with words and speech; they are won with action, you low caste *musahar*,' Krishna chuckled. 'And you along with other boys from our area will have to support me in this job.'

'Why should *we*?' Shiv made a face.

'Because my caste is ranked higher than yours, *musahar ke*,' Krishna mocked. Shiv was stunned by his reply momentarily and then both burst into laughter.

गूंगी धरती बोल रही, कच्चा चिट्ठा खोल रही
जागो रे मजबूर किसान, जागो रे मजबूर किसान
रक्षक यहाँ लुटेरा है, मुँह लटकाए सवेरा है
मुल्क उपद्रवग्रस्त इलाका, PAC का डेरा है
वोट की फसलें काट रहे, आपस में हिस्सा बाँट रहे
जर्जर होता हिन्दुस्तान, जागो रे मजबूर किसान

The mute earth eventually speaks to unearth its dirty hidden secrets
Rise up, you helpless farmer; rise up for your rights, you helpless farmer.
Who you thought is your saviour, is a bandit in disguise; what you thought was a bright morning, augurs sadness and anguish
Our land burns with disturbance and turmoil; swarmed with the camps of the police battalions
They play the politics of votes, to harness profits they divide within themselves
For the sake of our nation that goes decrepit; rise up you helpless farmer!

The street play was at its last stage, being enacted in the lawns opposite the University library. The students participating in it were divided into two groups, the oppressed farmers versus the tyrannical policemen and the powerful village landlords. The *sutradhaar*, or the emcee along with a group of singers chanted the script while actors performed, tied up to the screenplay.

The spirit of the sun had not dampened and every day seemed to be competing with the one gone by on temperature. Chhavi checked the microphone one last time as she signalled at the CSWI members to wrap up the play faster. The crowd had swelled up to about a hundred students who watched the play. The street play ended and the group merged within the crowd.

'Victimize the weak and uninformed; bully them to build power and profit for self. The rule of the land applies right here in our University as well,' Chhavi said, fleetingly looking across the crowd. The look on their faces reflected that they expected more.

'Four questions, *chaar savaal* is what we have,' she said waving her four fingers. 'For these so-called university heavyweights, Gope and Akhil Tiwari. The first I had asked a couple of days back, about backdoor admissions that have happened this year. Do you remember?' She could see a few of them nodding.

'I am going to ask the second question today. So how many of you are into any kind of sport in this university?' She could see about ten raised hands.

'What sport do you play for the university?' Chhavi asked a dusky complexioned girl wearing T-shirt and jeans.

'I am in the swimming team,' she responded.

'And you?' she asked two lanky boys who stood next to each other and had raised their hands.

'We play in the basketball team,' one of the two replied.

'Hmm...And what about you?' she asked a stocky student standing in the first row.

'I am a boxer.'

'What have you got from the student's fund for your teams this year? New sports kits? Any new gear?' She paused. 'Anything?'

The students looked at each other without making a sound. 'Do you guys know how much money has been allocated to sports in the student fund this time?' she asked.

'How much is it?' The boxer asked.

'10 lakhs!' The eyes of the listeners flew wide open. 'So if it's not coming to you, where is it going?' She put the final statement forward.

'Where are the funds going?' the basketball duo asked in unison.

'You need to ask this question to your current president Gope,' Chhavi said firmly.

'Madam, I have a question for you too,' Krishna's voice sliced the silence suddenly. Chhavi penetrated her sight in the crowd to trace the intruder.

Krishna cut through the semicircle that had been formed by the students from behind and walked right up to the front, to face Chhavi. He was followed by Shiv and about half a dozen of their ilk.

'Question for me?' she looked surprised to see a tall, athletic-built student wanting to ask her a question. She looked askance at Ravi, who nodded with reaffirmation.

'Who are you?' Krishna asked bluntly. 'The proctor, dean or the university vice-chancellor? Who are you, madam?' His voice became sharper.

Though taken up completely by surprise, she didn't lose her bearings, masking her tentativeness under a warm smile.

'None you mentioned. Perhaps your inner voice.'

'It would benefit you if that voice stays just inside and is not used to misguide this gullible lot. We all know what you CSWI lot are up to. Spread lies, sensationalize issues to grab the seat of power rather quickly,' Krishna said firmly.

'How can you say that these are lies, my friend?' Chhavi asked.

Krishna pulled away a bunch of pamphlets that a CSWI volunteer was holding in his hands to distribute and read it aloud for all to hear.

'They play with your future. They squander away the funds kept aside for your progress. They mess with your student rights day in and day out. They are the leaders who you have voted for in the past and they seek your support again. Will you reach out to these crooks again or bring in a change?' he read while distributing them across his companions.

'When you point one finger at someone, the other four point at you. Why don't you talk about the change CSWI wants to make rather than this half-baked truth about others?' he said and tore apart the pamphlets and threw the tiny paper bits up in the air. Ravi wanted to intervene, but Chhavi stopped him.

'You think you can prevent the truth from coming out?' she looked at the crowd that had lost its voice. 'How many times can you do that?'

'Every single time. You will find me everywhere,' he said and gestured at the crowd to disperse before walking away.

'Who was that idiot?' Ravi sniggered. 'And why didn't you let me stop him?' he asked while picking up the scattered pamphlets from the ground.

'No idea. But there was no point in a debate with him in front of the students. We would have looked like one of the other leaders who are always defending themselves as against fighting for the rights of these students,' she replied as she kept the pamphlets neatly back in the bag.

'We don't have to silence their ignorant voices; we just need to make them listen to their inner voice somehow,' she said.

'These are seasoned rogues, Chhavi. And some in the making. I doubt whether they have any bit of goodness left in them. They go and sell their souls to their so-called masters for a bottle of cheap liquor and personal favours,' Ravi remarked angrily.

'There's goodness in everyone, Ravi. It's for you to realize that and for him to discover it.'

'You are hopeful about everything, however bleak or impossible the situation might be. No?' he asked with a dash of sarcasm.

'If it wasn't for hope, we wouldn't have run again, after having fallen down the first time. No?' She smiled.

'Didn't I tell you guys that Krishna could do this?' Gope boasted as he took a swig of whisky from the cheap tea glass.

'Why not Gope bhaiya! For millions of years these guys have been doing the task of cleaning shit from our lives, our society. They cleaned some of it today from this University,' Abhay said sarcastically. Krishna and Shiv sat on the mat spread on the floor of the room while others were sprawling on the wooden cot.

'Abhay, today's been a good day. Why don't you give Krishna and Shiv something to drink as well,' Gope said.

'There aren't any glasses for these guys to drink from.'

'Take one glass and pour them a drink; they can adjust in one. After they are done, just throw it away, stupid. You don't have to use it again.' Gope laughed as if he had found a solution to the million-year-old caste dilemma.

Krishna and Shiv looked at each other and squirmed in discomfort. They had grown up with such assaults, yet it brought in a distinctive ache every time they were unleashed.

'What do you think Krishna? Will they have the balls to do their chaar savaal again?' Gope slurred.

'Even if they do, I will be there to stop it again,' Krishna said sipping from the glass that had been handed over to him.

'Hmm...yes, you need to do that. Everybody should be convinced that this is a gimmick by CSWI to gather sympathy votes. Clean politics? My foot!' Gope swore loudly and gulped the contents of the glass in one go.

'Bhaiya,' Abhay displayed his set of betel-stained teeth, 'if university is allowed to run by these self-confessed honest politicians, then where will people like us go?'

'I don't know about others Abhay, but you will go to jail for sure,' Gope said with a straight face and then the room erupted with laughter. Abhay looked grim at being the butt of the joke.

'Are we doing the right thing?' Shiv asked. Krishna was engrossed in reading a classic Hindi fiction called *Raag Darbari*.

'What's wrong in it?' He glanced at Shiv.

'You didn't answer my question. I mean, why should we be doing things that we are not supposed to do?'

'We are not supposed to clean shit of animals that belong to Yadavs, or work for zilch in their fields, wear clothes worse than their servants,' Krishna said excitedly and then checked himself. 'If we did all of that and got nothing, here, at least we will get something out of it.'

Shiv straightened the pillow under his head and sat upright, 'Get what, Krishna?'

'We will get an entry into Gope's camp. At least people would get to know low castes like us.'

'You are doing this for people to know us?' Shiv asked.

'Yes, at least the world should know that we have a name given to us by our parents, like them. We were not born as a chamar and a musahar.'

'That girl must be shocked with what happened in that meeting. Did you notice how beautiful she looked? Must be a Brahmin's daughter, no?' Shiv asked instinctively after a few moments.

Krishna chuckled. 'Why? Did god give Brahmins an exclusive license to produce gorgeous girls in this world?'

'It seems as if they are the only fortunate ones born with all the benefits. Good family, land, education, food, money and also the looks.' Shiv sighed.

'We will also have all of that one day, Shiv,' Krishna said.

'Can we have it Krishna?' Shiv asked, his eyes sparkling with imagination.

•

Radhey Shankar Mishra took the centre stage on the dining table whenever the family ate together; his chair was left vacant when he would be touring his constituency. Saraswati, his wife had left the world at a young age, and the kids became the sole responsibility of her old mother who had offered to help, realizing that Panditji's life would be in shambles otherwise. Panditji was more an adept politician than a father. The age difference between the eldest Vijay and the youngest Chhavi was merely six years. They had grown up together, holding each other's hands. Vijay was now into the business of road construction in Sitapur, Panditji's home constituency, and was gaining foothold in the area through his father's political clout. The younger one, Anil, had keen interest in politics and was honing his skills by working with the party members on the ground level. Panditji believed that Anil would carry his political legacy forward, Vijay would build the empire, and Chhavi would keep the values of the family intact.

'How is the work going Vijay? What's the progress on the Sitapur-Lucknow bypass?' Panditji asked as he took another helping of the dal.

'The tender is next week, Baba, and Ghanshyamji from PWD (Public Works Department) has assured us of full co-operation,' Vijay said mixing rice in his plate with the dal.

'Let me know if an intervention is required. I had helped Ghanshaym in that scam when he had siphoned off the land meant for agriculture, illegally. The agriculture minister was personally out to grab his neck. If he was not from our constituency, I wouldn't have massaged the minister so much to save that guy's ass,' Panditji said.

'He's indebted to you Baba. I don't think he will ever forget what you did for him,' Vijay said.

'It's good that he remembers,' Panditji stopped chewing momentarily, 'because favours are usually forgotten by the ones with an impure heart.'

'Baba, for how long will you be here?' Anil asked cheekily.

'Why? Do you want me to stay for something special happening in Lucknow?'

'Yes Baba. Haven't you heard of this new student leader who is really firing up the entire student community in the University?' Anil looked mockingly at Chhavi who gestured at him to maintain silence.

Panditji was engrossed in eating, 'No, I haven't heard. Who's that?'

'It's someone you know dearly, Baba. It's her.' Anil giggled and pointed at Chhavi.

'Chhavi?' Panditji looked surprised. One couldn't be sure of how he felt.

'Of course Baba, and look at the irony. I am elder to her and still haven't really addressed any political rally, while she is busy giving speeches in the University.'

'Anil bhaiya...this isn't fair,' Chhavi protested, not looking at her father.

'Why hasn't anyone told me earlier?' Panditji asked sombrely, looking at their Nani.

'There is nothing serious, Panditji,' their grandmother said, sensing anxiousness in the air. 'It's all a part of growing up in the college. Isn't it, Chhavi?'

Chhavi looked up at Panditji. 'Baba, I have joined CSWI. It's a new set up aimed to usher in change amongst the students. We want the University to run in a different manner,' she said measuring her words.

'CSWI, Revolution, Change. These words are not new; everyone speaks them fluently without grasping their meaning fully,' Panditji said.

Chhavi hesitated. 'Well... Baba, CSWI is different. We want the accountability and change to rest directly with the students. We are certain that no one wants to keep quiet once they know that their silence is harming them. We want to be the students' voice.'

'Didn't I tell you we have a budding leader here, Baba,' Anil said wanting to diffuse the seriousness.

Panditji spoke in a measured voice. 'I have given all of you enough freedom. To live your life the way you would want to. Treated you as equals unlike the manner in which our community looks at children. Chhavi, you are the precious one, and I want you to be no less than your brothers,' he said and took a sip of water.

'If Anil can enter politics, so can you, but one should be fully aware of the repercussions that politics offers,' Panditji paused to glance at Chhavi.

'Baba, I am not doing this to become a politician. The issues that CSWI has raised against the current system are valid. I empathize with them. I am a mere supporter who has got the opportunity to speak in front of the students and I am doing just that,' Chhavi said.

Panditji took a deep breath. 'I feel relieved with what you say but let me caution you Chhavi. Politics is known to suck everyone inside; even those standing at the periphery.'

The science department building was abuzz with voices and laughter at noon. It reminded Krishna of the sound emanating from beehives that hung like garlands on the trunks of banyan trees in his village. If you looked at them from a distance, it would seem that some million bees were up to something vigorously, and as you got closer, all you could hear was the hum of the hive. He walked towards the flight of stairs along with Shiv and a couple of other boys from the neighbouring villages who studied along.

'Hey Krishna, wait! What's the hurry?' His classmate Raghav called from behind.

'So you guys put CSWI in trouble yesterday, huh?' Raghav said. Shiv glanced at Krishna, who searched for an appropriate reply.

'It was not intentional, but what does one do when lies are hurled non-stop,' Krishna replied.

'How do you know they were lies? As far as I know, CSWI is really asking the right questions, that no one has yet dared to ask. Gope and others are all bloody crooks,' Raghav said disgustedly.

Raghav looked at Krishna, 'We have been together in this University for over three years now. I always thought of you as someone sincere having bright expectations from the future. The Krishna I saw yesterday was somebody else,' he patted Krishna's shoulder.

Krishna raised his eyebrow. 'Why? Is having a difference in opinion and raising your voice a virtue enjoyed by few here?' Krishna said, irritated.

'Having a different opinion is fine, but the manner in which you voiced your displeasure looked as if it was provoked,' Raghav said.

Krishna put up a fake smile. 'No one provoked us. Are you coming for the class, Raghav?'

'The lecture isn't starting now, it's been delayed by an hour. The professor is late. Let's go to the canteen meanwhile,' Raghav said. The sole five rupee note in Krishna's trouser pocket reminded him of his inability to accept the offer.

'No, we are expecting some friends here. You carry on,' Krishna said as they sat down on the stairs.

'What did I tell you Krishna? People will realize that what we are up to isn't natural, but a provocation,' Shiv said after Raghav had left.

'Huh! Who cares, Shiv? These guys have a problem even if we disagree with something,' he said.

'Why do you always have to make it us versus them? And a guy like Raghav wouldn't care much about caste,' Shiv said.

Krishna shook his head in disbelief. 'I don't believe it, Shiv. You are saying this! It's only here unlike any other place in the world that you are born with two identities – your religion and your caste. You may not have a name, but you will have this identity sticking to you like your shadow. Wherever you may go, it will walk with you, never leave you alone,' Krishna said staring ahead.

Shiv went silent but abruptly mumbled after a while, 'Who do I see there? Aren't they the CSWI party people?'

Krishna nodded. 'I think they have planned a meeting here, but I am not sure whether they will have one after they find us.'

'Trouble comes looking for us,' Shiv exclaimed. 'Let's avoid it today, Krishna. It will be too soon.'

'I won't be the one to start it, but if they do, I have given my word to Gope.'

Chhavi walked with Ravi and a bunch of their comrades towards the science department building. She walked cautiously as she carried the antique hand microphone in one hand and her handbag slinging on the shoulder. They stopped in front of the science building and looked around.

'There isn't much crowd here except the ones in the building shade and on the stairs. I guess once we start, it will pick up,' Chhavi said.

'Isn't that the same guy?' Ravi murmured looking in the direction of the stairs. Chhavi followed his gaze.

'Yes, that's the same bunch. Anyway, let's start,' she said casually.

'I have got some information on him. Krishna Kumar, first year M.Sc. He is known to be an easygoing guy, doesn't mix up much with others, remains with his own clan,' he said while taking the pamphlets out of the bag.

'Clan?' she asked.

'He is a chamar, so stays in the company of low caste students. Birds of the same feather flock together,' he snorted. 'It wasn't expected from him what he did yesterday. People who know him say so.'

'Perhaps he is being provoked by someone and he is doing this at their behest,' Chhavi said gesturing at the group to be ready for the street play.

'Maybe that is true. But why would a "nobody" like him do this. Liquor? Power? Or money?' Ravi asked distributing pamphlets among the CSWI volunteers.

'No one likes to be known as a nobody. And all of these – liquor, money or power – won't really help to change his status. So I don't know why he is doing it,' she said.

'Do you think it would be a good idea to do this elsewhere? These morons may want to create trouble all over again,' Ravi said.

'Running away from a problem will make it follow you even harder. Moreover, there is a reason behind every encounter in your life,' she said checking sound on the microphone.

Ravi looked puzzled. 'This encounter doesn't look pleasing, though.'

'Every encounter has the potential to change something within your life. So why would you shy away?' she said.

ख्वाब देखने का शौक हो तो उन्हें पूरा करने का जिगर रखो
अपनी मंज़िल पाने की अगर हो मंशा तो तपते कोयलों पर भागने की हिम्मत रखो
हत्यारे से अगर हो नफरत तो उसका छुरा उठते ही खुद का सीना आगे करने का दम रखो
भ्रष्टाचार से अगर उगती हो मन में कोफ्त तो उसके पेड़ को जड़ से काटने की कुल्हाड़ी रखो
दिल में अगर लेके घूमते हो प्यार तो उसे उगल भर सकने की दमदार आवाज़ रखो

If you fancy your dreams enough, then gather that courage to accomplish them
If you aim to reach your desired destination, then prepare yourself to run through the path laden with burning coals

> If you carry enough hatred in your heart for the assassin, then be ready to thrust your chest forward as he raises his dagger to strike
> If growing corruption torments your soul, then be prepared with an axe to bring down the tree of that malaise right from its roots
> If you wander around with a heart overflowing with love, then have the guts to spew it out when the time comes.

The chorus filled the corridors of the science department as the street play reached its crescendo. The actors moved around in a circle holding placards that had single words such as "Courage", "Corruption", "Victory", 'Love" written on each one of them. Chhavi cleared her throat and rehearsed her speech in the mind for one last time.

She greeted the crowd and began, 'My dear fellow comrades and students of this wonderful University. As many of you are aware, CSWI – the Common Student Wing of India – wants to usher a change in the way student issues and problems are being addressed here,' she glanced at the swelling crowd.

'It has been our endeavour to enable students to get what is rightfully theirs. But as we progressed in our search, we realized that there are provisions made year after year by the central government, state government and the University authorities to take care of many issues that you face,' she looked fleetingly in the direction where Krishna and his friends were seated.

'What we found out after a thorough check was that neither these funds and nor the provisions, none of it reaches you.

'It was at this time that we decided that as your representative, we needed to act on your behalf. We can't give you funds, or the provisions, but what we surely can get to you is right information,' she tried making eye contact with the crowd that listened with rapt attention.

'So we thought we will ask chaar savaal, four most important questions that impact the life and career of every single student studying here. We will question the leaders of Lucknow University Students Union, the leaders who were elected by you... and then see how they respond.'

She paused for a split second. 'Do you know how they responded?' The crowd kept absolutely still.

'Exactly like that! They responded the way you did just now. They are all silent,' she said emphatically.

'When a question is asked, we only keep silent on two occasions. Either if we have something to hide, or when we think that the issue is too irrelevant to respond to.'

She raised her hand and pointed at the student crowd, 'Anything that concerns you, the students, definitely can't be small. So?' she paused again.

'They are hiding something,' one girl amongst the crowd almost shouted in excitement.

'Exactly,' Chhavi exclaimed. 'So today our third question, *teesra savaal* to them concerns a lot of you who have come from far flung places with an earnest desire to study. For you to do that, the University needs to provide you with cheap hostel accommodation, but is that possible?'

She could hear faint murmurs as students got talking amongst themselves. 'We have 1200 rooms across our six hostels, including the sole girls' hostel. That means, considering double occupancy, the University can accommodate only 2400 students every year. Now let's factor in that a student in a normal course spends five years here... three doing his graduation and two for post-graduation. Am I heard?' she said. The crowd affirmed.

'Instead of five, let's take six years for one new cycle of 2400 students to exit after factoring in some students who fail, fall sick, can't appear for the exams, are doing projects, right?' she continued.

'So on an average, about 15-20% rooms out of 1200 rooms should be available every year. Am I correct?' she asked the students. She could see a lot of them nodding their heads.

'So, around 200 rooms should be made available to four hundred incoming outstation students every year. Do you know how many new students actually get into these hostels?' she looked at the blank faces of the students. 'Slightly less than a hundred students in about fifty rooms.'

'What happens to the other 150 rooms?' someone from the crowd asked.

'Your leaders and their cronies overstay for eight, ten or more years; rooms get allotted on fictitious student names; non availability of rooms is cited as reason as they connive with corrupt University staff members,' Chhavi said and from a corner of her eye could see Krishna rise and walk towards her.

'Aren't you and your party doing the same thing that you are blaming other leaders for?' Krishna yelled.

Chhavi's heartbeat ran faster. 'What is that?'

'Not giving credible information to students and misinforming them. Is that the ideology of CSWI? Divide and rule... or rather, mislead to rule,' he said.

'We don't act without facts, mister,' she stretched her hand towards Ravi who handed her a notebook.

'You don't seem like you belong to this city. Do you stay in a hostel?'

Krishna nodded. 'Yes. Subhash Hostel.'

'Room numbers 7, 19, 26, 29, 38, 40, 43, 47 from your hostel either have students who have spent more than eight to ten years in the University, or are being occupied by students on whose names the rooms haven't been originally allotted,' she said growing in confidence.

'Krishna, they seem to have done their homework well this time. Chaubey in 19, Dheeraj in 38, Trivedi in 40, and Dixit in 47 are all stalwarts languishing here from the day perhaps the hostel was inaugurated,' Shiv murmured in his ear.

Krishna resisted. 'Sarvesh stays in room number 26 and I am certain that the room was originally allotted to him. So is the case with Manoj in 7.'

Chhavi spoke firmly, 'We are certain about our facts. It would be better if you go back and check yours.'

Krishna looked troubled with his weakening argument. 'I don't need to get facts about my hostel from you,' he said pointing a finger at her.

Ravi, who had spent mammoth energy and time to unearth this information, was livid. 'This is the problem with guys like you. It's just because you can't win an argument on merit, you would want to win it through force. Your quota system doesn't work everywhere, not in a rational debate for sure,' he rattled unconsciously.

Krishna choked for a moment. Was it the mere sting of Ravi's words, the realization of being called a low caste in full public view... or a crude attempt of domination once again by a high caste individual? He strangely remembered that moment from his childhood, his class-teacher kicking him hard in the stomach, after he had accidently touched the water tap which was meant to quench the thirst of everyone else in the school, except a *chamar*.

Krishna glared at Ravi. 'What does it have to do with our caste? Why do you guys have to ridicule us over it all the time?'

Chhavi could see emotions running amok on Krishna's face. 'It's not what he meant. He just wanted you to look at the real picture. It's this conspiracy between the corrupt leaders and office bearers in the university that is leaving students high and dry. Ravi has toiled hard to unearth this correct piece of information.'

'No, he didn't say this. Let him say more vehemently that just because we don't belong to the upper castes, we don't have a right to speak, to debate with people like you on what is right and what isn't. You have controlled our past and now you want to do this to our present and future as well?' Krishna lashed out.

Ravi wanted to speak, but Chhavi silenced him with her eyes. 'We are not here to deal with anything else except student issues. So if you are keen to debate anything else, we are not game.'

'This isn't a debate; it's an attempt to douse our voices under ridicule that you carry in your heart against a section of people like us. We can do the same by not listening to you and falling prey to your false propaganda,' he said and snatched the bundle of pamphlets from a hapless CSWI volunteer.

'So, you want to shut us up through force. It won't work with me,' she said firmly.

'Neither will your attempt to ridicule our caste make us stop what we intend doing this time,' he said throwing the pamphlets up in the air and walking away.

'You shouldn't have mentioned it, Ravi. Our plea was getting so well received. The caste remarks made by you were a spoiler,' she said after the crowd had thinned.

'He was pitching his argument so aggressively in front of the students, I just completely lost it. These guys don't have the balls to open their mouths back in their villages, and then they come here to bigger towns and suddenly discover their lost voices,' Ravi was enraged.

'What you triggered in him today will make him all the more determined to stop us from what we want to do,' she said.

'What should our next move be? Stay quiet for a while?' Ravi asked.

'You don't abandon plans of going to a war just because you have a few battles to fight on the way,' she said resolutely.

'Krishna!' Shiv said. Krishna was flattened on the cot under a thin sheet that covered him from head to toe. He didn't reciprocate but Shiv knew that he was wide awake.

'It could have turned ugly today. I thought you would start a fight,' he paused and then nudged him with his foot.

'A fight would have meant that I was more upset with them calling me an untouchable rather than the student issues they were wallowing about. It would have shifted the cause that we were disputing,' he said from under the sheet.

Shiv was agitated. 'I was ready to explode the moment he called us a low caste in front of all the students.'

'Since the time our society was grafted, we have been forced to obey the upper castes, do the oddest job, and never question their superiority. If you ever tried to do that in the village, they would have bullied you with force; here they did it with their words. So nothing has really changed,' Krishna said.

'Weren't you livid with them as well?'

Krishna spoke from under the sheet, 'Not just with them. I am incensed with this world.'

It was rather late in the night when someone knocked on Chhavi's door. She put her books aside and got up to open the door.

'When did you come home Baba?' she exclaimed letting Panditji enter her room. Panditji smiled and then stepped inside. He glanced around the room and then stopped to gaze at her mother's framed picture that was taken in their farm at Sitapur.

'This was taken when you were less than a year old. It was election time and I was busy campaigning around Sitapur. Your mother had come over for a few days with all three of you.'

He turned towards Chhavi. 'How was your day at the University today?'

'It was good Baba,' she said.

He picked up one of her books from the table. 'I checked with my sources today. The elections fever is hotting up in University. Gope isn't going to give up his seat easily; he is a tough one and wants to go a distance in politics. He is also one of those who won't bother much about the means to get where he wants to.'

'I am aware Baba, but what he wants has no concern with what the students want,' she said.

'Lok Shakti doesn't support Gope and if you would ask me personally, I disregard these University elections as a principle. You are too young to realize that politics is not just about quick money and power. So once you get used to it in the university, you can't live without it once you get out into the world,' he said.

'I have gathered some information about your party, CSWI. You guys have good intentions, but no ideological base to support you. There is an imminent danger of people like Gope to prey on weaker ones like you.'

'We are not weak, Baba. Enough work is being done right now by our comrades to tell these guys like Gope that their days are numbered. We will throw them out,' she said hastily.

Panditji looked at her intently. 'I can sense the level of your involvement in the University elections and politics. That was not the reason why you had gone to the University. No?'

Chhavi unlocked herself from his gaze. 'But I can't be completely oblivious of my surroundings, Baba. I owe some responsibility to myself, to the society that I am a part of.'

'You have a responsibility towards us as well, your family. That comes first, Chhavi. I don't want any repercussions of your stint in University politics to spill over you or the family,' he said sombrely.

'I might appear harsh to you at the moment, but you must realize that I have your best interest in my heart. I have been in politics long enough to know what a dodgy quagmire it is,' he said lovingly.

'If you are at the edge of it, then there still lies a chance of you being pulled out; but if you have walked deeper, then recovery is impossible,' he said looking at her. Chhavi maintained silence.

'Good night. Hope you don't forget what I just said,' he said.

'Like everything else, I will remember this as well, Baba.'

Gope was unusually edgy in the morning after having heard what had transpired the previous day. The plan of disrupting CSWI had kind of worked, but not in the grand manner that he had envisaged. There had been disruption and confusion during the meeting, but not dissonance against what CSWI claimed was being practiced by leaders like him in the University.

Abhay looked at Krishna who sat squatting on the ground, 'Why did you let her start the meeting in the first place? You shouldn't have let it happen.'

Krishna gazed at Gope, 'Bhaiya had said not to use force; to only upset the proceedings. If we would have used physical force, it would have become apparent that we have an agenda to stall their meetings. Anybody could have put the pieces together.'

'Who asked you to use intelligence that you don't have *abey chamar ke*?' Abhay was seething with anger. 'Now who will go and complete your unfinished task? I had warned you before using these good for nothing guys bhaiya,' he looked at Gope and said. Krishna hung his head low; anger and helplessness were turning into sweat, erupting all over his body.

Gope yelled in anger at Abhay. 'Just shut the fuck up Abhay. You are good for nothing except picking up squabbles at critical times with wrong people over stupid issues. What can Krishna do about it? Would he be shooting them with bullets when my brief was to only use words?'

Abhay was taken aback with Gope's stance. 'Bhaiya, I have given my whole life to you and now I have to hear this in front of these scoundrels.' He stared at Krishna with unadulterated hate.

Gope was in no mood to soften. 'So what should we do to reward your loyalty? Agree to your suicidal ideas and put our political career at stake?' He looked at Abhay gloweringly. 'At this time what was expected from people like you, is to come up with a solution to douse this growing fire. But you won't do that and instead add more fuel to it.'

'I won't utter a word now bhaiya, unless you ask me to,' Abhay muttered and looked in the other direction.

Gope shook his head in disbelief and sighed. 'When is their next meeting Krishna? We need to adopt a different tactic there, a more aggressive one. If plain talk isn't helping, perhaps some fear would.'

'Geology department, day after tomorrow at 1.00 p.m.,' Krishna said.

'Hmm.' Gope scratched his head and went into deep thought. 'Isn't there some protest planned that day against reservation as well?' He looked at a grumpy Abhay who looked the other way. He then shifted his gaze at Bittu.

'It's a follow up protest to the age old Mandal agitation, that never seems to subside,' Bittu nodded. 'Now that the quota has been implemented some years back for SC, ST and backward castes, these new scams keep unearthing time and again.'

'What is the new fraud now?' Gope raised his eyebrow.

'What bhaiya, you are our president and you don't even know what's happening right under your nose?' Bittu took a jibe. Gope smiled perhaps for the first time that day. Krishna looked up curiously.

'Fake caste certificates, bhaiya. To get admissions in undergraduate and postgraduate courses in medical colleges. The certificates have been sold at a price to non-deserving students who secured admissions last year on the basis of these. And they were not one or two, but over a hundred.'

'Hundred? That's quite a lot. So more than hundred deserving ones couldn't get admissions due to this and they are venting their anger against reservation?' Gope said.

'Yes, precisely! People usually vent their anger on the cause than the incident at such times. They will burn the reservation court order copies; some students may also attempt self-immolation for propaganda, but then not to die but just for impact... media attention and all that,' Bittu said.

'Then their friends and others from the crowd will stop them. Hmm...,' Gope said.

He stared at his feet for a while, thinking. 'Can we send a message to CSWI, and more importantly to Panditji's daughter, that politics is not just about making speeches... but a very risky road to travel on,' Gope murmured.

'What exactly do you have in mind?' Bittu asked.

'Throw some petrol on her. No one will notice this amidst commotion. It will be enough to scare her and freak Panditji out. He will ensure after this that his daughter never enters the CSWI office again,' Gope spoke menacingly.

Abhay's eyes were transfixed on Gope. 'Who will do this? Krishna?'

Gope looked at him unimaginably and shook his head. 'You will never learn, Abhay. Everybody by now knows that Krishna is against CSWI. Panditji will get him arrested and then they will unearth tracks that lead to me,' he pointed at himself. Abhay looked the other way after getting doubly wrapped.

'Bittu, you get this done from someone else. Okay?' Gope looked at Bittu who complied with a nod. Abhay winced as he looked at Krishna.

Krishna spoke hesitatingly, 'Bhaiya, I hope this won't turn dirty and also we will achieve what we want to.'

'There is one crucial thing that separates a body doused with petrol and a blazing one Krishna; that is fire. But on this occasion, we will replace fire with fear. Fear will be a powerful message to her and everyone else in CSWI that politics is not everyone's cup of tea. It will be enough to shake her off politics completely,' Gope said firmly.

Krishna nodded. 'You understand politics much better than me. Can I leave?' he said getting up. Gope nodded.

'Let me know what needs to be done next,' Krishna said.

'Abhay,' Gope said after Krishna had left. Abhay was still reeling under public embarrassment.

'While Bittu arranges for the petrol, you get the fire,' Gope said, his eyes glowering.

Abhay jumped from his seat. 'Fire? Did you say fire, bhaiya?'

Gope looked at him and nodded, slowly. 'There won't be a better opportunity than this. Student agitation and fervour at its peak, and amidst all of this, we will carry our task quietly.'

'What if she gets burnt?' Bittu asked palpating with nervousness.

'Even if she gets some of the fire, it would be enough to ward her away from CSWI and politics completely,' Gope said.

'Why didn't you disclose this to Krishna?' Abhay asked.

'Some plans have to rest closer to the heart. He is new and a Dalit...can't be trusted.'

'What if this news goes out?' Abhay muttered.

'There are only five of us in the room,' Gope gazed at the other two men besides Abhay and Bittu, 'and all of us want to live long,' he said coldly.

Tagore Library was located in the heart of Lucknow University. It was at noon when Krishna and Shiv entered the white coloured aesthetic building that housed about a million books covering diverse subjects from all over the world.

'We could have continued our studies in the hostel. Why have you pulled me here?' Shiv complained.

Krishna looked at him. 'Will your whining ever stop? Don't you like coming here with so much of unbridled peace, knowledge all around?' Krishna scoffed at him.

He then took a deep breath looking around. 'We are going to miss this, once we are out of the University. You can't even dream of such a place back home. No?'

'It's all right; this is just a building with many books. I don't find it useful beyond that,' Shiv said uninterestedly gazing at the giant glass book cases.

'Like so many other things that you have, but don't find them useful?' Krishna asked.

'Like what?' Shiv quizzed.

'Your non-functional brain, idiot,' Krishna burst into laughter. The librarian noticed the noise and looked sternly in their direction. Krishna tendered an apology through a gesture.

'Let's sit there,' he pointed at a group of vacant chairs in a corner.

'What do we plan to do here?' Shiv asked settling down on one.

'Oh Lord Shiv, your namesake here, is a complete nerd. The wisdom of mankind is around him and he asks what should one do? Didn't you grant him some brains before throwing him into this world?' Krishna mocked.

'The caste that Lord Shiv granted me at birth doesn't come with brains,' he smiled satirically at Krishna.

Krishna went speechless and then let out a half-smile.

'What do you keep writing in that diary of yours? Why don't you read it out to me sometime?' Shiv said looking at Krishna's diary that he had pulled out.

'There will be a day, when I will show this to you and to the entire world,' he said with a serious expression.

'Amen,' Shiv replied as he walked towards the book case.

Krishna kept his cotton bag on the table; it had been his companion for the last three years. Krishna opened his diary; it was choked. He had virtually occupied every single inch of space within it with his scribbled poetry and verses. There wasn't a geometrical pattern to how he wrote, top to bottom or left to write; he just aimed to fill every blank space with his words. It didn't matter if they didn't follow the conventional mode that the world followed. All that mattered to him was that each diary would cost him twenty bucks and he had to use it fully. He fiddled with his pen glancing at the library entrance. Chhavi Shankar Mishra entered with a small bunch of friends. Krishna's first reaction was to duck instantaneously, not wanting to get noticed by her.

'I am going to read Shakespeare today, since you praise his writing endlessly. How is this one?' Shiv said and thrust a copy of *Macbeth's* Hindi translation in front of him.

'It's one of his best works Shiv, very good,' Krishna replied, looking into his diary.

'I know all that, but what's the story all about? Can you give me a gist?' he asked.

'Why don't you read it yourself? Shakespeare would have spent years in writing it and you want me to convey that essence in moments,' he muttered irritatingly.

'Isn't that Panditji's daughter? CSWI's Chhavi Mishra?' Shiv had also noticed her in the library now. The group of girls stood in front of a history bookcase, busy discussing something passionately.

'Why don't we mind our own business? Let's not draw their attention towards us,' Krishna almost pleaded.

Shiv did not seem to hear him. 'These Brahmin girls are born with such good looks, Krishna. Just look at her, a nymph from heaven, a soothing balm to the troubled heart,' he spoke almost like a poet.

'Shh... Just shut up, Shiv!' Krishna hushed angrily and looked towards her. It was a moment he didn't know then, he would remember all his life. There wasn't anything more beautiful that he had ever seen before, her biscuit coloured skin looked flawless like the moon, albeit without its dark spot. The hair reminded him of the dark midnight that he gazed at, lying down on the cot in front of the pond, behind his house in the village. She had a smile that stretched from one end of her face to the other, as if it would never shrink back; just like Goddess Radha's in the village temple, where she stands with Lord Krishna. Krishna at that moment felt that Chhavi was God's gift to this world.

It took a tap on his shoulder to bring him back to the present. 'You are the most unexpected one to be found in the library.'

Krishna turned back, never expecting her. He squirmed before unwanted words popped out, 'Why so madam? Since when has the library become an upper caste property?'

'You need to relax a bit. I think you have taken the other day's conversation to your heart. Trust me, I don't endorse it and apologize on my colleague's behalf,' Chhavi said at once. Shiv meanwhile was frozen in his seat.

'Hello, by the way. I am Chhavi,' she introduced herself to a blanked out Krishna.

'My name is Krishna,' he said.

Chhavi smiled and glanced at Shiv who sat next to him. 'He is my friend Shiv,' Krishna added.

She looked around. 'You guys come here to study regularly?'

'Yes, one is usually here to study, madam. They sell tea in the canteen,' Krishna said wryly.

She laughed heartily. 'Oh! So you possess a sense of humour too. Good to know that.'

'Is that too a privilege granted to a select few?' he remarked sarcastically, again.

She smiled. 'Listen, that's enough Krishna. I have apologized for what happened the other day. Let's keep our debates for the CSWI gatherings, okay?' Krishna was reminded of Gope's plan, due for execution tomorrow. He felt a sudden pang of anxiety.

He nodded and got up to avoid any further conversation with her.

'Studies over?' she asked.

He couldn't find an appropriate reply. 'I am thirsty, need to drink water,' he made an excuse.

'No need to disrupt your studies for that. Here, take this,' she pulled out a plastic water bottle from her bag with stars printed all over it.

Krishna stared at her and the innocuous gesture. He was speechless for a moment.

'Take,' she said again.

'I... I can't drink from this,' he said as he looked at an equally flabbergasted Shiv.

'Why? Come on, take it!' She thrust the bottle in his hands.

Krishna took off the cap nervously and looked at her once again. She was inattentive and made small talk with her friends. He held the bottle over his mouth at a distance, took a sip, then the second and almost finished the entire bottle. The water tasted better than ever.

'Thank you,' he said handing it back to her.

'No problem. Bye, see you again.' She smiled and gestured at her friends to leave.

Krishna and Shiv stood there transfixed for a few moments before walking out of the library.

'Krishna, this was a miracle,' Shiv said. They would have walked for a couple of kilometres before he spoke. Krishna kept walking.

'A Brahmin girl offering water to a chamar, from her personal water bottle, even after knowing which caste he belongs to,' Shiv said breathlessly. Krishna kept silent, taking rapid steps.

'Isn't this a miracle?' Shiv grabbed him by the shoulder.

'Yes. Just like us, all of them aren't bad,' he said.

'What about tomorrow? It's going to be a rough day for Panditji's daughter,' Shiv said.

Chhavi squinted at the sun. 'An afternoon to get roasted in. So damn hot today.'

The CSWI teams had gathered in front of the Geology department building and were busy running through the act for the day.

'We don't have time for the street-play today, so we just raise our placards during the time Chhavi makes her small speech. Ok?' Ravi ran through the instructions. The CSWI comrades nodded.

'The reservation protest march should be here shortly. I expect a lot of ruckus and vapid sloganeering. We should be finished before then,' he looked at Chhavi and said.

'Yeah, I won't be taking long today. Just take some student feedback and that should be enough,' she said and tapped on the microphone.

'Yeah, take feedback from your favourite admirer, that Krishna as well in case he walks in,' he said.

Chhavi giggled. 'Oh! I forgot to tell you. I had bumped into him yesterday in the library. He could barely speak there, and look at the way he reacts in public!'

'That's because guys like them can lead mobs but won't fit into places where civil people flock,' Ravi muttered heatedly.

Chhavi snapped, 'You shouldn't be speaking like this Ravi. It's just because such a feeling exists within people like us that they have never been able to enter the mainstream. Imagine their anger and frustration at being deprived for hundreds and thousands of years for basic human respect and dignity.'

'So, does that mean you will come and snatch a job from me on the basis of your caste and not your competence?' Ravi asked, not softening up.

Chhavi glanced at the crowd that was growing. 'That's an altogether different debate and can continue till cows come home. But for now, just believing that we are equals and hence require similar respect and empathy should be enough. Anyway, let's begin,' she said.

'Good afternoon, fellow colleagues and friends. Warmest Greetings from CSWI – the only party in the University that aims to usher in clean politics amongst students like you and me, having no political agenda.'

She continued, 'That's why we need a leader and a sincere party who is one amongst us to know about our problems and our issues. We don't really expect them to solve our problems, but become a platform for us to raise our voices; be our voice-hearers who can then in-turn make them heard to the people who matter.'

'Today, I will not be asking any tough question to my fellow elected leaders, so there won't be the fourth question or the "*chautha savaal*" for them. We shouldn't make them paranoid. Let's allow them to relax a bit, no?' She smiled. She could hear some loud chuckles from the crowd.

'So, instead of them, I have a question for you today. What is that one single thing that you hate in this University? That one thing that really makes you angry and sick towards everyone who is involved in running this place?' She gazed at a couple of hundred faces that stared at her curiously.

'Rampant and blatant eve-teasing,' a girl standing extreme left in the crowd lashed out.

'Ramshackle canteens,' another voice said loudly.

'Pathetic bathrooms, insensitive law and order, lesser number of lectures,' the answers started flowing out like a clogged drain being cleared free, after days. In the midst of noisy voices filling the air, Chhavi saw Krishna walking towards her from the Social Works department, the next building.

'Your best friend is back to create more trouble,' Ravi mumbled into her ear. Chhavi looked at him reassuringly, that she would be able to handle the situation.

'Do we have any more concerns?' She asked and glanced towards her left to see a procession heading towards the Geology department.

'I think the protest march is here,' she hushed. Ravi gestured at her to finish it off quickly.

'Hostel food sucks, too many blackouts during examination, street lighting in the campus,' the voices and the grievances were showing no signs of stopping. She signalled at the CSWI volunteer who was noting down the complaints in a notebook to hurry up.

'Okay friends, thank you for letting us know about your issues. We have taken a careful note and will try to address the action points against each in our subsequent interactions with you. See you again,' she signed off rather hurriedly.

The protest march carried along a multitude of students. They reached the Geology department and were quickly realigning in a huge circle. The participants chanted loud slogans against reservation, the scam that happened under the guise of reservation, and the state government's apathy towards it. CSWI members were pushed into the front row of the circle as they had been there from before.

'Should we leave?' Ravi mumbled into her ear.

'We might learn a thing or two from them. Let's watch,' she said.

In a matter of few seconds, about a dozen students moved to the centre of the circle, each carrying a protest placard with them, which they waved frantically in the air. They signalled at another group who waited in one corner to come inside the periphery of the circle. The sloganeering had picked up a feverish pace and hundreds of students raised resounding chants against reservation in the air:

बड़ा अमंगल मंडल है, छात्रों का ये दंगल है
बुद्धिमान यहाँ ठण्ड से है मरता, मूरख के पास कम्बल है
हाय हाय मंडल, हाय हाय मंडल

The Mandal reservation is a curse for students; who fight the bout of their life
For because of it, the intelligent die of cold; as it protects the foolish with a warm blanket
Down with mandal; down with mandal.

Amidst the ruckus, a few students in the centre pulled out bottles of kerosene and started spraying oil on themselves as they walked around briskly in a circle.

'What are they planning to do?' Chhavi asked alarmingly.

Ravi dismissed her concern by a wave of his hand. 'Oh! It's just for effect. They won't do anything to themselves,' he said and pointed at a few cameras that were suspended in the air, marking the presence of media journalists.

Just then, Chhavi could feel something watery fall on her, tricking down rapidly over her forehead, rolling over her nose, the whiff was intoxicating and familiar. Her brain processed in a moment that it was petrol. She turned around instantly, but by then the act had been committed a second time over, and this time a much higher volume of petrol soaked the upper part of her body. She looked around in disbelief and couldn't notice anyone who would do that; everybody seemed to be absorbed in the ongoing drama, raising slogans against reservation. Some of the petrol fell on nearby students as well who didn't seem to notice amidst the noise.

Chhavi shook Ravi's shoulder fiercely, 'Someone here is spraying fuel aimlessly, let's leave.'

Ravi looked shocked to see her dripping. 'What the hell is this? Who did that?' He looked around annoyingly. He could see Krishna in the crowd looking towards them.

'Are you sure it wasn't that Krishna?' Ravi said all keyed up.

'No idea Ravi. Let's leave first.'

They turned around to leave. No sooner had they taken a few steps that Chhavi felt a deep burning sensation on her right side.

The group standing on that side suddenly jumped away from their position. 'Look at this girl! She has set herself on fire,' one of the rally supporters shouted.

Chhavi froze watching the right hand side sleeve of her cotton kurta; it had caught fire as the flames leapt over, engulfing the sleeve inch by inch, within a fraction of seconds.

'How did this happen?' She screamed. Ravi was shocked, too numb to react.

'Help me!' were the only words that came out of her mouth as she looked at her burning arm, the ruthless flames devouring the cotton and then pouncing on her naked flesh to spread over it with lightning speed.

The protestors saw this as a god-sent opportunity, more interested in cashing the moment than saving an unknown girl.

'Look at her torment, what has made her attempt this, shows her anguish against reservation,' a reservation placard holding student shouted.

'Somebody, help her!' One of the girls in the rally protested. The voice jolted Krishna, who was in shock till then with this disastrous change in the plan that he had no clue about. Fear was the only feeling they were supposed to leave her with, not this pain and torture. Anger ran through his veins and before it would explode his brain, he had jumped over her.

The panic of watching fire over her body was now turning into a severe burning sensation. The flames were at work furiously. And then suddenly, someone was all over her. She was knocked down on the ground when someone tried to douse the fire on her by chafing it with his shirt sleeve. The petrol changed sides quickly and some of it got rubbed off on his shirt also. She looked up once in panic and pain, surrounded by an uncaring crowd that chanted selfishly, and then she saw Krishna.

He was trying hard to thump the flames with his bare hands, on her arms and back, and in that process, getting soaked in petrol too. She could see helplessness on his face as he fought to douse the flames, but sensing no improvement, eventually he removed his shirt and pushed it hard against the flames. It worked, for the flames quickly started losing their sheen. But nobody in that frenzy noticed that the petrol on his bare chest and stomach had caught fire. Krishna could sense the pain, but strangely felt relieved to see her getting free from the ravaging flames. He saw a bucket of water being hurled on Chhavi by a bystander, when someone shouted, 'He has fire on his body. We need more water.'

Chhavi stood there shaken with the experience, drenched in water and feeling a severe burning sensation on one side of the body. She desperately wanted to scream for help as she saw his bare flesh burn, but the voice stuck in her throat refused to listen. He desperately tried to whack the fire from his body with both his hands unsuccessfully, before he shrieked with pain and fell down on the ground. The last thing Chhavi remembered before passing out were buckets of water being splashed on Krishna as he lay there unconscious.

'A Dalit coming to the rescue of a Brahmin girl and saving her from getting torched? All hell would have broken loose, sahib?' Ram Singh asked a pensive KK.

They sipped tea at a highway dhaba just a few miles ahead of Malegaon. It was about five and the evening itched to be set free from the receding afternoon.

'Yes, it was. A chamar rescuing a Brahmin girl from her self-immolation bid against reservation was the "Breaking News",' KK said. 'No one cared to find out that it had been a deliberate attempt to harm her. There was more juice in the other story, so that became the talk of the town.'

'I didn't know that you are from my state, Bihar,' Ram Singh exclaimed.

'Ram Singh, my past is here,' KK pointed towards his heart, 'and it has always stayed there. Would you have worked for me even after knowing that I was a Dalit?' He glanced at him.

'Sahib, the two biggest adversities that one can be born with in this country are caste and poverty. I am not from a dominant caste either; and like you, have inherited both these merits.' He smiled wryly.

KK could fathom the similarity between their hearts. 'Which district are you from?' he asked.

'Samastipur, Sahib,' he said and then asked abruptly, 'Are you going to meet Chhavi madam in Lucknow?'

KK was a tad surprised. 'How did you know Ram Singh?'

'I know Sahib. It's in your eyes. Why didn't you meet her earlier?'

'I had promised her,' KK said.

'You had promised not to meet?' Ram Singh asked.

KK nodded as he gazed at the gaping highway on which vehicles of all shapes and sizes raced together, blowing horns, racing against each other towards their own unique destinations.

Krishna opened his eyes slowly and stared at the white ceiling for a few seconds before regaining his memory. He lowered his gaze and amidst dancing dots of black and white that blurred his vision, he could see Shiv sitting next to the bed where he lay. It appeared to be the general ward of a hospital where patients were packed like sardines on neighbouring beds. They looked uncomfortable with the disease, the syringes that poked their frail bodies, and the hostile environment in which they had been dumped.

'What's the time?' He strained to ask.

'It's been a day since you have been here. It's three in the afternoon!' Shiv replied.

A drip was inserted into Krishna's arm that felt numb, but his chest burnt as if it were still on fire.

'How did I come here?'

'Our guys picked you up and got you admitted here,' Shiv said.

'What's the news?' Krishna whimpered. Shiv handed him the day's news paper silently, 'Third page.'

When adversary turns into a saviour – A Dalit student saves a Brahmin girl from torching herself in the reservation protest.

Krishna read it twice, thwarting various feelings that raced in his mind. He started reading the article.

Today in Lucknow University, the bastion of student politics, history was written. Students, hundreds of them, were protesting against the illegitimate admissions happening in medical universities across the state due to bogus caste certificates being issued to non-Dalit students. The protest was in its full force when some students frustrated with the apathy of the government, got excited enough to think about the extreme act of self-immolation as a mark of their anger.

It is reported that a girl named Chhavi Mishra, daughter of the stalwart Lok Shakti leader Pandit Radhey Shankar Mishra was also a part of the Mandal Reservation protest march. She decided to take this acute step too, along with others, and tried self-immolation. In an unprecedented manner, she was saved when the fire on her body was doused by an unknown Dalit fellow student, a couple of years her senior from the university. The name of the student is reported to be Krishna Kumar and he belongs to the Darbhanga district of Bihar. The student fraternity and the entire city is intrigued by this act where a Dalit has gone and risked his life for a Brahmin girl who was protesting against misuse of reservation being handed to backward castes. The boy has been hospitalized and his condition has been reported as stable.

The state administration has taken a strict cognizance of the situation and security has been beefed up in the University.

Krishna read the article and looked at Shiv who waved a bundle of the day's newspapers in front of his eyes. 'Do you want to read more? Lord Krishna,' he mocked.

'Why do you speak like this?' Krishna asked.

'Do you have any clue about what's happening outside?' Shiv asked irritatingly. Krishna stared at him with a blank expression.

'Gope is livid. He doesn't know why you did what you did. First we oppose CSWI, disrupt their meetings, and then you go and save that girl in front of the world like a hero,' he muttered heatedly.

'Why did they change their plan, Shiv? We were supposed to scare her, not burn her alive,' Krishna spoke with trouble.

'They didn't do that Krishna. It wasn't a part of Gope's plan. Now with what you have done, even Dalit boys are taken aback.'

'You have made it look as if we are supporting these high caste crooks by saving that girl,' Shiv shook his head out of frustration.

'I don't know who else could do it if not Gope. I just couldn't stop myself when I saw her grappling with flames,' Krishna said feeling the thick bandage on his chest.

'This altruism of yours has cost us, dear. Neither can we go back to Gope or clarify to our natives about this dramatic change of your heart,' Shiv mocked in frustration.

'Whatever people know and all that is written here is fake,' Krishna threw the newspaper towards Shiv. 'They wanted to harm her and that too real bad.'

'All that is written here may be fake, but not what you did. That was real,' Chhavi said standing right behind Shiv.

They had been oblivious to her presence, engrossed in their duel.

'When did you come?' Shiv got up from his chair, startled.

'Just entered,' she said as both Krishna and Shiv heaved a sigh of relief for her not being privy to their entire conversation.

Krishna looked at her arm cushioned under a bandage and said, 'Hope you are fine. No major injuries to worry about.'

'The major injuries have been taken care of, by *you*,' she pointed at his chest.

'Please sit,' Shiv offered her the chair. She quietly sat on it and looked at Krishna.

'Is it very painful?' she asked.

'Yes it is. Like burning charcoal on the chest,' he said.

'Can I see it?' she asked.

Krishna gestured at Shiv, who pulled the sheet down till his waist. The bandage was soaked with turmeric-coloured antiseptic and ran all over his chest and stomach. She raised her hand over the bandage and gestured to bring it down slowly.

'Don't touch,' Krishna blurted. His clan was averse to a touch from a high caste.

'I won't hurt, don't worry,' she said touching him gently.

Krishna could feel her touch even beneath the bandage that ran a couple of inches thick; it was soft and reassuring.

'Why did you risk your life for me Krishna?' she asked.

'I don't know. I just did what felt right at that moment,' he said. Chhavi waited for him to speak more, but he didn't.

'My father Pandit Radhey Shankar Mishra wants to meet you, Krishna. He wants to thank you,' she said.

'I will come to meet Panditji once I am out of here,' he said.

'When will the hospital let him go?' she asked Shiv.

'They will be keeping him for a couple of days,' Shiv said.

'Ok. Thanks once more for everything that you did. Here are some fruits,' she handed over a large bag that seemed to contain fruits and other eatables.

'Baba is here for only three days and then he would be travelling to his constituency. When should I tell him that you are expected?' she asked.

Krishna looked at the day printed on the newspaper, it was Tuesday. 'Friday. I will come to meet him in the evening. Shiv, can you drop her to the gate please?'

'That's fine. I will manage,' she said while turning back and walking out of the door of the general ward.

Shiv spoke a few minutes after she had left. 'It was nice of her to come here. The hearts of these upper castes are usually devoid of any gratitude towards people like us.'

Krishna was silent.

'What do we tell Gope when we meet him?' Shiv looked worried again.

'No idea,' Krishna replied staring at the roof.

The pain had not completely left Krishna's body, yet he decided to meet Gope as soon as he was back in the hostel. It was better to face him sooner than live with anxiety.

He limped a bit as he entered Gope's room with Shiv. Gope's face looked glum and his expressions did not alter after noticing them.

He measured him from head to toe. 'Have you recovered, Krishna?'

'Yes bhaiya, I am fine now.' Krishna kept standing. Gope gestured at the mat on the floor, but Krishna shook his head.

'It pains more if I sit, bhaiya. I would rather stand,' he said.

'If you can't tolerate this bit of pain, then what was the need to become a hero in front of the world? Bloody chamar ke?' Abhay sitting amongst them saw this as a perfect opportunity to lash out. Gope gestured at him to cool down.

'What were you thinking Krishna when you jumped in the fire to save that girl?' Gope asked.

Krishna didn't speak. 'I am asking something Krishna. Give me a reply!' Gope raised his pitch.

'The plan was to get the girl scared, not murder her bhaiya,' he spoke in measured words.

'We didn't do it, didn't I tell you that we only wanted to scare her,' Gope retorted looking at Abhay.

'Bhaiiya, I was there. I saw it with my own eyes that it was a deliberate attempt,' he said.

Gope then looked into Krishna's eyes. 'Even if someone did this knowingly, why did you have to save her?'

Krishna looked at him with disbelief.

'You shouldn't have poked your dirty nose inside. Even if the bitch would die, it wouldn't matter. I would have at least got rid of that one thorn,' he screamed.

Rage gripped Krishna's body as he heard this. It was strange that he wanted to harm Gope that very instant, but he curbed his inner desire.

'You didn't ask me to stand there and watch her burn,' he said.

Gope stood up and walked towards him. He pierced his finger into the bandage that wrapped Krishna's chest. 'I didn't ask you to save her either, bloody chamar.'

Gope had punctured both; his wound and his heart. He winced in pain momentarily and then turned back to walk out. Shiv stood behind, dazzled with the sudden happenings.

Abhay gripped his shoulder, 'You are disrespecting bhaiya by showing him your back. Should we teach this bastard a lesson?' he sought Gope's permission.

'Let him go. I had some hopes from him, but he turned out to be useless. Now with what he has done, he is left with nothing. There isn't anyone left with him now, neither us and nor his own clan who thinks he has gone renegade,' Gope said.

'You should take the road back to your village now,' Abhay snarled.

'Bhaiya, I will stay here only.' Krishna looked at Gope.

'Never dare to cross my path again, Krishna,' Gope said raising his index finger. Krishna nodded before he left the room along with Shiv.

'What if he opens his mouth bhaiya? That he was working at our behest,' Bittu said.

'Who will listen to him? If he is of no use to Gope, then he can't be of any use to anyone. He is a waste, leave him alone,' Gope said coldly.

Krishna opened the cupboard and took out one of the three shirts that he had. Luckily, it was ironed. Shiv was lying down flat on the cot and stared blankly at the ceiling fan that made noise, as if ready to fall down any moment.

'What will Gope and his bunch of cronies do next? What if they try to harm us? As it is we are outsiders here,' Shiv said.

'Low caste outsiders,' Krishna added looking at him.

Shiv turned away. 'Aren't you scared of them? First you screw everything up and then you walk out instead of making a truce.'

Krishna buttoned up the shirt carefully, guarding the bandage on his chest. 'I want you to hear this story Shiv.'

There once lived a king who had such a beautiful queen that it was said that no woman in the entire world could match up to her beauty. One day the king had a strange dream that someone eloped with his wife to an unknown land, leaving him desolate and wretched. The next day when the king woke up, awful fear gripped both his body and mind.

'What if this happens in reality?' Just the mere thought made him tremble. He decided to lock up the

queen in a secret section of his palace under security and round the clock surveillance. The queen resisted, at first gently and then reminding him about her status and then of his foolishness.

'It is just a dream, dear husband,' she pleaded.

'But what if this dream turns into a reality,' he said without budging from his stance and imprisoned her.

The queen was not used to living without her husband and in loneliness and isolation. She became irritable initially and soon after stopped taking her meals. In a couple of months, she had become frail and looked twice her age and then soon a day came when the most beautiful woman in the world passed away.

Krishna sat down on the chair, 'So?'

'What?' Shiv asked.

'Fear of the uncertain future inhibits you to live fully in the present. The king became so fearful that instead of choosing to live in pleasure with his wife, he let the fear of future cripple him. It gave him nothing but took away the only thing he cherished the most, his wife,' Krishna said.

Shiv was staring at him blankly. 'What has happened in the past is gone, Shiv. Both of us can't do anything about it. But what we do in the present will certainly determine our future. If we keep moving ahead with fear in our heart, then future isn't going to be pleasant either,' he said walking out of the door.

Panditji took a long hard look at Krishna as he entered the living room of the palatial bungalow. He had never ever set his foot before in a plush house like that. Krishna could only draw a comparison with the houses that belonged to Yadavs, in whose fields his father laboured and their animals that his mother tended. Even their large pucca houses dwarfed in comparison to the one that he was standing in, intimidated with its splendour and sheer size.

'What did you say your name is?' Panditji's voice broke his trance.

'Krishna...Krishna Kumar,' he replied hesitatingly. Pandiji gestured at him to sit on the plush sofa that lay there.

Krishna was non-decisive for a few seconds and Panditji could gauge his dilemma immediately, 'Take a seat Krishna. We are not one of those who believe in this discrimination. Being in politics for so long has erased this divide from our minds altogether.'

Krishna was sucked into the comfort of the sofa as soon as he rested on it.

'Where is your native place?' he asked.

'Jalegar, District Darbangha, Bihar,' Krishna replied not looking at him directly.

Panditji looked sideways and shouted, 'Can someone call Chhavi over here?'

Panditji cleared his throat, 'What you did that day to save our daughter from getting hurt requires a lot of courage and that is a virtue that's in a real short supply in our times.'

Krishna smiled weakly. 'People most often will think twice before doing it for their own ilk and you did this for a stranger. It is something rare. I wanted to see this young man and offer my heartfelt gratitude,' he said and patted Krishna's shoulder. Krishna acknowledged Panditji's gesture with a gentle nod and kept looking down at the marble floor that sparkled under the artificial light emanating from the majestic chandelier that hung from the ceiling of that dome-shaped room.

'Oh, Krishna! When did you come?' Chhavi entered the room smiling and sat next to her father.

Krishna looked up once to see her beautiful form and then shied away from her gaze, 'A couple of minutes back.'

Panditji turned his attention towards Chhavi. 'I would have loved to sit long, but some guests are expected any moment here. Why don't you take him inside and serve him some snacks and tea?'

'No Panditji, I better get going,' he said getting up.

'You can't leave without having something. I insist,' Chhavi said forcibly. Panditji gestured at Krishna to accept the invitation. Krishna relented and started to follow Chhavi to the neighbouring room.

'Krishna, wait! Just come here for a moment,' Panditji said. He turned back as Chhavi had walked into the other room. Panditji pulled out a stack of five hundred rupee notes from his pocket and offered it to him.

'Panditji, if I would have done this for money, that's the first thing I would have asked from you. There is no need for this,' he said looking directly into Panditji's eyes, perhaps for the first time.

Panditji paused briefly. 'I like your attitude, Krishna. It will take you far in life.' He patted him again. 'Any idea of who would have plotted this? Though Chhavi blames it on chance, I smell a conspiracy here.' Panditji's years of accumulated acumen did not want to accept this as a mere stray incident.

'I wouldn't know Panditji,' Krishna said as Panditji kept the bundle of currency notes back into his pocket.

"Why don't you have one?' Chhavi picked up a samosa from the plate and gestured at Krishna who was sipping tea. Krishna nodded as he glanced around the room. Everything seemed expensive and huge to his eyes. The dining table itself would have been bigger than his house that gave shelter to four.

'You belong to Bihar, no?' she asked.

'How do you know?'

'It was mentioned in the newspapers,' she said and gestured at the plate again.

He picked it up consciously and took a bite. They tasted fabulous and more so when they came free of cost.

'So where have you schooled from?' she asked.

'There is a government school near our village. All the kids from neighbouring villages go there,' he said.

'Who else do you have in your family?'

'Father, mother, Ganesh my younger brother and Gauri, our buffalo,' he said. Chhavi smiled instinctively.

'Is your father a farmer?' she asked.

'Yes, he is, but works in the lands that belong to Yadavs. My mother works at their house,' he said immersed in finishing off the last bit of his samosa. Chhavi paused, sensitizing herself to the reality of his life. She picked up the plate and gestured at Krishna to have one more.

'What will you do after college? Any plans for the future?' she asked.

'If I choose to listen to the world, then I should be trying for a stable government job. But if I choose not to...' he paused and kept the samosa back in his plate.

Chhavi looked at him with soft eyes. 'What do you really want to do? Right from here,' she said pointing at her heart.

Krishna glanced around, unsure of revealing his desire. 'I want to write, and my desire is to be known for it.'

'I know my Hindi is not the purest and besides knowing the basics of English I am not good at that either,' he said after a pause.

'I don't know about English, but you speak Hindi pretty well. At least that's what I learned when you argued with me in the University.' She smiled.

He smiled wryly. 'Yes, I know the language, but Bihar oozes out of it whenever I open my mouth.'

'That's fine Krishna. There is no reason for you to be embarrassed about your roots. It gives you that uniqueness that differentiates you from others,' she said.

'Even if the source is surrounded with filth and is ugly?' he asked.

'Yes, like a lotus flower that blossoms from a muddy pond. Like you said you want to be a writer, this native experience can be the edge in your writing,' she said. 'Can I see something that you have written?'

'I don't think it is worth of your reading, but I will show it to you nonetheless,' Krishna said.

'Isn't that for me to decide if it's worth or not?' she asked. Chhavi's words comforted him.

'I should leave now. Thank you for the snacks and the tea,' he said.

'Wait! I will be back in a moment,' she said and disappeared in her palace.

She reappeared and handed him a book.

Krishna read the title. '*Love Story*! My English is not good enough for me to grasp this.' He hesitated.

'It's written in extremely simple English. You will be able to...otherwise take the dictionary's help,' she said. He nodded.

'When do we see your writing?' she asked.

'Whenever you may want to,' he said. She smiled.

'What happened to the bypass tender?' Panditji looked up after pouring some curd in the bowl. He had been unusually quiet that day at the dining table as everyone ate silently.

'We got it Baba. Ghanshyamji helped us in the end,' Vijay said.

'Good, I like men who have enough gratitude to repay their old debts,' Panditji said.

'What is the value of the tender?' he further asked.

'It should be around two-and-a-half crores,' Vijay replied.

'Send something to Ghanshyam,' Panditji said.

Vijay looked surprised. 'Baba, you have already done so much for him. Wouldn't it be more than required if we send him a gift as well?'

Panditji raised the bowl of dal to his mouth and emptied it fully. 'A few lakhs wouldn't mean so much to you, but for him, he would sink further under your obligation. If you don't give him anything for this deal, he would assume that his previous debt has been repaid and he is free.'

Vijay nodded.

'The two greatest fears in a man's life are the fear of debt and the fear for people whom he cares for. These two don't leave him even for a moment,' Panditji said.

'You are right Baba. I will get this done,' Vijay said thoughtfully.

'How is your village contact program progressing Anil? Are the boys exerting themselves?' he asked.

'Yes Baba, there are five teams that are out each day, seven days a week, trying to understand the problems in each village. Then we work with the local Sarpanch and administration to see if they can be resolved,' he said.

'The problems may or may not get solved; that is a separate issue. But people should see that you are dirtying your hands in their affairs,' he paused. 'People living in villages are a very different breed than the ones who live in cities. Just like they don't forgive easily, they don't forget either.'

Panditji's gaze shifted towards Chhavi who gulped water from the glass. 'Is your wound completely healed?'

She nodded. 'Yes Baba.'

'I suggest that you leave your experiment with student politics for the time being and focus on your studies,' he glanced at her along with her grandmother.

'But Baba, I can't leave CSWI in the middle and walk away because of an accident,' she resisted.

'It was not an accident Chhavi, but an attempt to harm you. I am trying to find out who the culprits are,' he said.

'I have a responsibility towards CSWI. I can't leave them hanging in the middle,' she said.

Panditji coughed once. 'You have a responsibility towards the family first. You will have to choose between us and CSWI,' he said coldly. Her grandmother wanted to say something, but Panditji gestured at her to stop. The dining room was drowned in silence for a few moments.

Chhavi got up from her chair, 'In that case, the family wins Baba,' she said and left the room.

'Aren't you coming for the class?' Shiv said buttoning his shirt. Krishna was covered from head to toe with a sheet that fluttered over his mouth due to his breath. Shiv glanced at him again and repeated his question.

Finally he grasped his feet and shook them. 'Are you sleeping?' he asked.

'No, flying a kite,' Krishna muttered half-asleep and uncovered his face. 'There is some bug in these medicines. I have been feeling drowsy all through yesterday.'

'We have hardly any time before the class starts. Coming?' Shiv had moved on to combing his hair looking into the small mirror that hung on the wall.

'The chest still hurts; I don't want to take a chance. You carry on. I will rest here only,' he said.

Krishna kept lying on the cot for a while after Shiv had left, thinking about how tumultuous the past few days had been. Old friends had turned into foes while the ones who appeared to be foes earlier seemed like friends now. The visit to Panditji's house had been warm and meeting Chhavi was perhaps the encounter that he had waited all his life for. Finally he had met someone who did not want to judge him on the basis of his surname, but for what he was. He picked up the book kept on the table that she had loaned him and started reading it. Strangely, the English looked simpler than what he had thought, and even if some words didn't make sense instantaneously, reading the full sentence made him understand the gist of what the author wanted to say. He progressed slowly and in about an hour, he had finished six pages. Not bad, he thought. Six minutes to a page.

It was about one in the afternoon when he heard a knock on the door. 'Who is it? The door is unlocked. Come in,' he said raising the decibel of his voice. There wasn't a reply, except a knock again. He turned the book upside down and kept it on the cot, got up and opened the room door. He was speechless to see Chhavi standing there.

'How are you feeling now?' she asked.

It took him a few seconds to realize that this was for real. 'How come you are here Chhavi ji? How did you find my room?' he gasped.

She smiled. 'Why do you say this? Am I not allowed?' she said and peeped into the room over his shoulders.

'No, no. I didn't mean that Chhavi ji. It's just that this is a boy's hostel and you could have called for me somewhere more suitable,' he stumbled with the words.

'Is there a "No Girls Allowed" sign somewhere that I can't figure out?' she mocked in good humour.

When Krishna stood stupefied, she said, 'And stop calling me "Chhavi ji". Chhavi wthout a "ji" sounds just fine.' Krishna nodded.

'Won't you allow me into your room?' she asked a flustered Krishna. He stepped away from the entrance, giving her space.

'So this is the place where the writer stays,' she said glancing around. Krishna quickly picked up the used towel from the cot and dumped it into one corner.

'How did you find my room?' he asked again, still reeling under the unexpected scare she had given him.

'One can succeed in finding God if he seeks him with a sincere heart. You are a mere mortal Krishna.' She smiled.

'No, I didn't mean that. Not many people know me in the University, that's why,' Krishna said hiding his embarrassment.

'Believe me, it's not so the case anymore. The newspapers have made you famous,' she said. 'Who do you stay with?'

'Shiv, the one who was with me in the library the other day,' he said gesturing her to sit on the chair.

She sat down and turned back to look out of the window. 'It's so hot outside. Is this enough for you?' she was looking up at the rickety old fan latched to the ceiling.

'That's fine with us. We don't have the luxury of even this back home,' Krishna said.

She squirmed in her seat. 'So let's see some of your writing.'

'Are you sure, Chhavi ji that you want to hear it? It may look pretty amateurish to you,' he said.

'Listen, I had told you earlier that no ji please. And as far as your writing goes, it's for me to decide,' she said with mock irritation.

Krishna pulled out his diary from the cotton bag and stretched it out towards her. 'Most of it is poetry and some short stories,' he said.

'You need to read them out, mister,' she said. Krishna hesitated for a moment and then flipped through the pages, stopping at a page to start reading.

खो सी गयी है आज की भूल भुलैया में हम हल्की फुल्की बातें
आज की भारी हवा में तो हम मुँह ही नहीं खोलती
हाल चाल पूछना, घर की खबर लेना, शहर का माहौल पता करना
उन्हें भूल कर हम खो भर गयी है पेचीदा मसलों में
संजीदा खबरों में, भयानक हादसों में
और बिखरते रिश्तों में
करो थोड़ा नाश्ता हमारे साथ कि हम फिर मुँह से फूटें
कुछ चुस्की लो हमारी कि हम फिर से बहें
नाराज़ भी हो जाओ कि गलियों में हम निकलें
लेकिन अगर चुप रहोगे तो हमें क्या कहोगे
अपने दिल और दिमाग भरे रखोगे तो हमें क्या सुनोगे
हम तो तैरती हैं हवा में आस पास तुम्हारे
बस पकड़ो अपनी मुट्ठी में और ले आओ अपनी दुनिया में
खुश होंगी हम और हँसेंगी तुम्हारे साथ
रंगीन कर देंगी तुम्हारी हर पल बेजान होती दुनिया को

'It's wonderful Krishna. What a splendid thought! Deep and excellent use of words,' she clapped gleefully with both hands.

'I am glad you liked it Chhavi ji...umm sorry... Chhavi,' he said looking embarrassed with the praise.

'That's better. Can we hear some more?' she asked.

'Okay fine. One more,' he said gaining confidence with her praise.

उन सपनों से क्या रिश्ता जो सोने न दें
उस प्यार का क्या किस्सा जो रोने न दे
उस दिल का क्या भरोसा जो बसने न दे

उन पलों का क्या इंतजार जो जीने न दें
जब सब कुछ ठहरे तो कुछ आने की चाह क्यों हो
जब सब कुछ खो जाये तो कुछ पाने की परवाह क्यों हो

'This is a short one, the last that I had written,' he said and shut the diary.

जब सब कुछ ठहरे तो कुछ आने की चाह क्यों हो
जब सब कुछ खो जाये तो कुछ पाने की परवाह क्यों हो

She repeated the lines once again. 'Brilliant! What makes you think that this is written by an amateur?'

'I don't know. Never thought that I could write something that would be worthy enough,' he said.

'Do you have something to eat? I mean like some snacks. I am hungry,' she asked.

'We don't keep any, just cook meals here,' he said plainly. 'Snacks are expensive.'

Chhavi recollected her composure. 'That's fine too, what is there for lunch?' The small pleasures in our lives that we don't even give a second thought are special to many.

Krishna looked at the electric stove placed on a small stool next to the door. 'We should have some rice and dal here,' he said. 'If you want, I can cook that,' he said. Chhavi nodded, smiling.

Krishna added some turmeric and salt to the soaked dal in the small pressure cooker kept on the electric heater. 'This will take about ten minutes, and then I will make the rice. Unfortunately we can't make both of them together.'

'That's fine. I will be able to survive till then.' She smiled.

'You won't be used to eating just rice and dal. We don't have a vegetable today,' he said.

She didn't want to lie because she was actually not used to that food. 'Don't you eat in the hostel mess usually?' she asked.

'It doesn't suit our pocket. We can't afford to,' he said. Every layer that he peeled off from his life exposed how different their lives really were.

'Krishna, will you tell me something about your life, childhood and your family?' she asked.

'Do you really wish to know? I mean, it will be very different from any of the stories that you would have heard or read,' he said looking at the lentils boiling within the pressure cooker, bit by bit.

I was born in Jalegar, a quaint little village in Bihar in a Dalit family. At the time of the birth of a newborn in a Dalit's family, there is a tendency to name him after a god. Do you know the reason?' Chhavi shook her head.

Gandhiji used to call untouchables the children of god. So it became prevalent to name Dalit babies after some god. Like I was named Krishna at birth. But over the years I have realized that it is perhaps not the only reason. After having led a life of extreme poverty and discrimination, they hope that by naming their child after a god, he may perhaps act like one when he grows up. Maybe he has the power to transform their lives along with others down the social ladder, like only a god can.

My father worked as a labourer in the fields of Yadavs, who are not exactly high caste, but much more distinguished than us, the chamars. There is a pond in our village on one side of which are all the high caste houses - Brahmins, Kshatriyas, Baniyas, Yadavs and the others; while on the other side is where the muck resides - that is, all the Dalits like us. The pond has clean water all the year round and also fish. The high-walled houses of the high castes are beautiful, made with concrete, stone, and clay-tiles. The high castes have lush green patches of land where they grow crops and vegetables varying according to the season.

The other side of the pond is where people from low castes stay in houses made of mud and thatched roofs. The entire village is not very clean, but dirt and filth seems to multiply manifolds in the patch where we stay. Naked kids, pigs, stinking shit in the drains was the environment that I grew up in and soon lost my averseness to it. Baba worked in the fields from early morning till evening wearing just a dhoti. When the afternoon sun is on your head, cutting the bunch of wheat is an extremely tough and painful task. The ground feels as if you are standing on molten lava and the roots of the cropped plants pierce the flesh of your feet like thorns. The roots belonging to lentils such as mustard hurt even more. So many times in my childhood I would know that Baba was inside the house by looking at the blood that he left behind on the porch of the house. Even his blood was not enough to feed a family of four each day. I don't remember a single day in my life when I have eaten to my heart's content, not even a day.

Chhavi was listening to him intently, her facial expressions changing with everything that Krishna said.

Amma also worked in the Yadavs' houses as a cleaning help. She worked from early morning till late afternoon, cleaning their cowsheds and then their houses. The months of winter were especially painful. The cows and the buffaloes would be tethered in the hallway and the floor covered with dry leaves of cane or straw to protect the animals from the winter chill. The dung and the urine of the animals would be spread all over the floor through the night, the stench of which would be so unpleasant that it would make one faint. Amma, amidst all of this would pick up their dung each day and bring it out for making dung cakes and also feed the animals alongside. The compensation for doing all of this every day was about twenty-five kilos of rice in a year, two pieces of flour rotis mixed with husk. This food was our meal every day unless a marriage in the village was in the horizon. Every Dalit would wait for a marriage like a farmer would wait for rains. After a lavish meal in the marriage ceremony, the guests carried their leftovers in leaf plates outside and handed them over to Dalits for their consumption. We carried them back home in large straw baskets, with leftovers sticking to them, to begin our feast henceforth. The uneaten pooris and vegetables would then be heated in a bit of oil and relished by our families. We would sing praises of those who had left behind the leftovers and curse the ones who had cleaned off their plates depriving us of such delicacies.

The Government High School in Bajitpur was the only school present near our village Jalegar. When I was young, I would often walk down to its gate and spend hours looking at the children studying inside with awe. Baba, during one of his visits to the market, saw me clutching the iron gate of the school; captivated with the happenings inside. He pleaded with Yadavs, his employer to help in getting me admitted.

'Why do you want to send him to school?' the elder Yadav asked.

'Sahib, perhaps his life would be a tad better than mine after studies,' Baba replied.

'Do you think he will grow up to be a collector?' the younger Yadav guffawed. I could see Baba wince, squatting on the ground.

They would have been in a good mood perhaps that his plea was heard, and I was admitted to the Government High School soon thereafter. I was overjoyed with the prospect of studying, thinking that life perhaps would now take a better course. My happiness was short-lived, for even after seeking an entry like other kids in school, my education would be quite different. I along with other kids belonging to low castes would be made to sit behind everybody on the floor where the floor mat didn't reach. Sometimes, it would get difficult to figure out what was being written on the blackboard and to hear what the teacher taught, but then we could never complain. The headmaster Kali Prasad was a demon incarnate – dark like a buffalo with protruding lips and enlarged nostrils – who took a special liking towards Dalit kids, especially towards me. He would often instruct us to sweep the ground with a broom as the other kids studied peacefully with no one bothering them. This torture went on for days as we were pushed to sweeping the ground and empty classrooms, till one day when I decided to resist. Kali Prasad was livid with rage and catching me by the neck, he threw me on the floor in front of the entire class.

'Bloody, chamar ka! It was insane of me for doing you the favour of making you walk inside the school gate,' he roared.

'Master Sahib, I am ready to do everything that you ask me. Please let me study,' I said with tears rolling down my cheeks.

'Bloody mother fucking chamar, you wait there till I get my stick and shove it up your back-side. How dare you refuse me?' he said violently. I remember walking down quietly to the ground with the broom in my hand in front of the speechless students of my class.

The pressure cooker whistled for the third time. That made Krishna switch off the electric heater.

'I think this is done. We can make the rice now,' he said.

'Did you complete your studies in the same school then?' she asked.

He smiled wryly as he emptied the dal into a bowl. 'There wasn't an option for me. Either I had to study there or nowhere.'

Everyone seemed to hate us and had some or the other problem with us. If one of us wore slightly cleaner and well-ironed clothes to school, we had to hear taunts such as – 'Look at this chamar ka, he is wearing new clothes today.' If we wore a shabby piece of clothing they would say – 'Don't come near me you stinking pig.' It was as if they hated us existing with them in their world.

The number of things which we couldn't touch in the village were far too many. The school tap, the walls of the temple, the well in the village, a high caste, their utensils. They would pat and touch their animals freely but not us, for we were worse; a curse to the high caste society. At the end of each year, Baba would plead the Yadavs to hand over the old books of their children to me. They would relent a few times, trading them against the grain that they gave us in lieu of the work we did for them.

Days such as these turned into months and then into years, each of these years awarding me with countless scars that I carry with me in the present. I may have left Jalegar behind by thousands of miles, but these memories keep burning within me like a fire. After finishing school, there wasn't any hope that I would be able to pursue college, but Baba decided to sell the other buffalo that we had - Bindiya. He took a decision to risk the survival of our family against not letting me pursue further studies. Baba wants me to walk further in life more than any of our low caste brethren; that's his only desire left.

The pressure cooker whistled again, signalling that the rice was ready for consumption. Krishna took out two plates from the cupboard and kept them over a newspaper that doubled as a tablemat on the cot. He put some rice in both the plates and put the bowl of dal next to them.

'A Brahmin eating food made by a Dalit and in his utensils is enough to cause a furore,' he said.

'I don't think people care much about it in cities,' she said.

'I have lived in this city long enough to know that most of them really do, like all of them in the village,' he said and gestured at her to pick up the plate.

'Sometimes a simple meal is just the right thing to eat,' she said mixing rice with her bare hand.

'There is a story that my grandmother used to tell me often when I was a child. Do you want to hear it?' she asked. Krishna nodded with his mouth full of rice.

It is the story of an egg, a carrot, and coffee beans. The three of them when put into hot boiling water behave absolutely differently.

The hard surface of the egg when put into boiling water comes out with its surface even harder than before. The rigid carrot when dipped into boiling water comes out pretty soft when pulled out. The coffee beans on the other hand behave very differently.

The coffee bean when put into boiling water not just changes its texture, but also gives it a wonderful fragrance and aroma. My grandmother compared egg, carrot, and coffee-bean to three different categories of people in this world, and boiling water to intense challenges and a hostile environment. The effect of hardships on people, who are like egg, is that they emerge more uncaring and snooty after the experience; more resentful towards the environment, hardened more than before. People who are like carrots look tough from the exterior, but as soon as exposed to hard times, their inner potential fizzles out and they transform into someone who they are not. Lifeless, defeated people.

It is only people who are like the coffee bean who have the ability to alter not just their circumstances, but also their environment, the effect of which can be seen by everyone around, just like the aroma of the coffee bean. All three of them are thrown into the same boiling water, but the way they respond to it is entirely different.

It totally depends on us what we want to become: an egg, a carrot or the coffee bean. Your upbringing has been in a very hostile and tough environment which has led to this angst building up within you, for years. Now the onus lies with you Krishna. What do you want to change, the environment that you can't or yourself that you can.

Krishna kept staring at her thoughtfully. 'What should I do to get rid of so much of negativity that has accumulated within?'

'Try becoming a sieve. Let go of all negativities and prosecution complexes inside and build on the wonderful inherent potential that you have, like your writing and the courage to fight the odds,' she said.

'Also finish reading this book and after this many others,' she picked up *Love Story* and smirked.

'I will finish this for sure. Thank you for coming here and talking to me. I already feel better,' he said.

'Me too Krishna,' she said.

Krishna was walking down the steps of the Science department when he met Shiv on the way. He was completely worked up.

'I was looking for you all over,' he said hurriedly.

'Didn't you know I was attending the class?' Krishna said.

'Chhavi ji wants to meet you,' he said breathlessly. 'She is outside the science canteen.' Krishna nodded looking at him and walked towards the canteen.

He saw Chhavi standing in the corridor with her back facing him.

'Did you call for me?' he asked.

She turned around looking all excited. 'Yes. Can we go out please? I don't have any more classes now.'

She had this knack of turning him speechless either with her sudden appearance or with words. That moment was no exception.

'Go out? I mean where?' He fumbled.

'Anywhere, but out of here,' she said. Krishna followed her out of the University to the main road where they hired an auto.

'Bada Imambara,' she said to the auto driver.

They sat in silence till the auto had taken a right turn from Parivartan Chowk and was crossing Hotel Clarks Awadh.

'Have you ever been to Bada Imambara before?' she asked. Krishna shook his head.

She looked at him disbelievingly. 'If you haven't seen Imambara as yet, what have you been doing in Lucknow?'

'We leave the campus rarely. Everything costs,' he said plainly and turned his gaze to the other side.

She bought the entry tickets from the ticket window and they entered the monument through a large archway. The red stone-laden path had beautiful gardens on both sides. The afternoon sun had started receding and with lush greenery around, the heat didn't hurt as much.

'Bada Imambara was built by Asaf-Ud-Daula, one of the Nawabs of Lucknow in the 18th century. There is a very interesting story behind it. Do you know?' she looked at Krishna.

'How would I? Have never been here before,' he said looking ahead.

She dismissed his indifferent remark. 'It is said that a famine had hit the city at that time which continued for a decade. So to save people from dying because of hunger, he started constructing this.'

'How did it save people?' Krishna asked.

'They were paid for constructing this, thousands of them every day. So whatever they constructed during the day, the nobility, or the rich during those times would dismantle it at night. The cycle of construction and then destruction followed by reconstruction continued till the time the famine lasted, which was pretty long, ten years,' she said.

'He would have been really generous to do that for saving people from starvation,' Krishna said looking at the magnificent main building.

'Yes, he would have been. He saved so many lives that were in danger during that ten-year spell,' she said.

They walked inside the main building that resembled a huge vault. Krishna looked up at the ceiling that seemed pretty high. A small group of foreigners stood near them listening with rapt attention to their local guide.

'Please listen to me carefully gentlemen and dear gentlewomen,' he spoke in broken English. 'This hall is fifty meters in length and sixteen meters in width. The height that you see from the floor to the ceiling at the top is sixteen meters with no support of beams or pillars, making it one of the largest arched constructions in the world.' The foreigners gasped in wonder as they looked up.

'It's really amazing to do this without a support,' Krishna said.

'What else is here?' he asked.

'The *bhul-bhulaiya*, upstairs,' she said, 'an incredible maze of corridors.' Krishna gave her a perplexed look.

She held his hand and pulled him towards the staircase. Chhavi's touch on his skin was electrifying, like the first shower of rain that brings a quiver to the body and then soothes it to the core.

'You know, there are about a thousand labyrinthine passages in this dark and dense maze? They are so confusing that if one gets trapped here, it can last for hours,' she said excitedly, climbing up the stairs. Krishna was more conscious to her touch than her words.

They walked through one of the narrow alleys on the first floor that opened above the central hall.

'This maze has several staircases that run up and down across various narrow alleys like the one we walked through.

Some of these alleys open up here at the central hall, some at steep drops, while others at dead ends,' she said.

Krishna was listening to each word attentively.

'So, one needs to be very careful while walking around this maze. I like the adventure here but minus these dark and narrow alleys,' she made a face and released his hand from her grip.

'Is bhul-bhulaiya on this floor only?' he asked.

'No, on floors above this as well, all connected through staircases. Do you want to explore?' He nodded.

'Well then let's do that, but you don't leave my hand. Ok?' she said innocently and took his hand again.

They climbed the staircase that led them to an alley and after walking a few steps, they reached a dead end. They turned back to take another one, but that also ended abruptly. Every narrow alley looked the same and after struggling to find a way out for a few minutes, it seemed as if they were walking through the same path repeatedly.

'There isn't a point in both of us just blindly entering any alley. There are four more ahead,' Krishna said stopping before one and pointing at the others. 'Let me go and find out the one that leads us to the platform above the main hall. I will be back in a jiffy and then we can take the right way.'

'It isn't so easy, Krishna. This is a maze and you will get lost,' she said.

'Give me a moment, I will be back,' he said and walked ahead.

'Don't enter the alley Krishna, you will be lost in this labyrinth. I will be left alone here,' she sounded upset. Krishna turned back and smiled feebly, her face looked troubled.

He looked inside the third alley; it looked brighter than the previous ones. It meant that it opened somewhere that had sunlight and not into a dead end. He walked ahead. One alley led to another, but there wasn't a sign of an opening. He turned back and from whatever he could remember, tried to take the same route back, where she waited. Chhavi wasn't there, so either she had moved away, or he was standing at the wrong place. He entered the alley anxiously and picked up his walking pace. Krishna's anxiety compounded with every passing moment that he walked through the darkness.

'Chhavi....Chhavi,' he shouted in the pervading stillness. No reply. He shouted again, twice, thrice and then many times. He had started sprinting through alleys now, his mind growing numb with every passing second. He saw a strong patch of light on the right hand side which made him rush towards it.

'Don't! You are going the wrong way, son. Watch out,' someone gripped his hand firmly enough to stop him in his tracks. Krishna turned around to look at him. He was the same guide who had met them in the central hall. The Japanese tourists were standing behind him, staring at Krishna as if he was a new discovery in the monument.

'There is a steep fall just a few steps ahead. You would have hurt yourself, son,' the tourist guide said and led him a few steps ahead where the alley ended. Krishna looked down; the fall would have been about a hundred feet. He could have had multiple fractures or perhaps died. He didn't care about himself as much as for Chhavi in that moment.

'I am lost. I have lost my friend too,' he said.

'Is she a lady?' the guide asked. Krishna nodded.

'I just guided her out of this maze. I will take you there as well. You need to be very careful out here. They don't call it bhul-bhulaiya just like that,' he said.

The guide signalled at his entourage to stay put for a few minutes and then asked Krishna to follow him. He deftly moved through the unknown alleys as if they were his lifelong abode, and before Krishna could regain his composure, they were in the gigantic balcony that looked down into the central hall. Chhavi stood there teary-eyed looking sideways when Krishna emerged from the darkness.

'I told you Krishna, you will get lost,' she said. Krishna avoided her gaze to look at the guide whose face was lit with a smile after having fulfilled his job.

'I am sorry for being hasty and leaving you there alone. I was terribly tense as well,' he said.

She walked a few steps ahead to inadvertently hug him. 'Don't ever do this again.'

Krishna was unsure of such moments that kept revealing themselves one after the other, unannounced, since the time that he had met Chhavi. He just didn't know how to react as they unfolded.

'I am sorry. Let us leave,' is all that he could say.

The guide expected some reward in return for his service, but neither did Krishna have enough money to give him, nor sufficient guts to ask Chhavi for it. They got down from the staircase and were back in the main hall again.

'Isn't there more to see here?' he said breaking the silence after a while.

'Haven't we seen enough?' she said. He could see a streak of anger running through her face.

She gathered her composure back. 'The Nawab who built this, Asaf-Ud-Daula is buried here,' she said pointing towards a canopy that covered a simple grave. 'There is a mosque outside where prayers are offered on Fridays and on other auspicious days. Do you want to go there?'

Krishna shook his head. 'Let's go back.'

'Baba wants me to leave politics and CSWI,' she said as the auto rickshaw was crossing the Gomti Bridge. The evening breeze was strong, causing the strands of her hair to fall repeatedly on her face that she pulled back with her index finger. Krishna silently wished if he could be allowed to do that.

'He would be concerned with what happened in the University that day. After all, he is a father as well,' Krishna said.

'But that doesn't mean that I don't do what my inner calling is,' she resisted. The auto-rickshaw stopped in front of the University gate.

'If I can be of any help to CSWI, I am ready,' he said.

Chhavi looked pleasantly surprised. 'You of all people will help CSWI?' He nodded.

'Why would you want to do that?' she asked.

'There are no answers to certain questions, so one should go with what the heart says,' he said.

'That's good. You write so well, and that could be of great use to CSWI,' she said.

'Well then. Bye,' he said after a brief pause and turned around to walk into the University gate.

'Krishna!' Chhavi called from behind.

'It's my birthday tomorrow,' she said.

'That's good news. It's a day for you to celebrate with your family.'

'Yes it is. Baba invites a lot of people in the evening to celebrate my birthday,' she said. 'Are you free in the afternoon?' she asked hesitatingly. He didn't reply and waited for her to speak.

'I want to go to a restaurant with you, for lunch,' she said. He looked uncomfortable and she sensed that the monetary implication troubled him.

'It's my birthday, so it will be my treat,' she said.

He was comforted. 'I won't be able to take you to a restaurant on my birthday.' He smiled.

'You can cook a meal for me in your hostel room at least,' she replied smiling.

'Chung Fa is a Chinese restaurant in Mahanagar. 1.00 p.m.?' she asked.

'I haven't heard of this place. How will I find it?' he asked.

'It's in Gole Market. Anybody will help you locate it once you reach Mahanagar,' she said.

The gigantic Tata Safari waded its way on the non-cemented road to halt in front of Chung Fa in Gole Market. Chhavi hopped out of the car looking at her watch; she was late by fifteen minutes. The restaurant was dimly lit and she squinted to figure out the dining area. Krishna sat quietly in one corner, looking visibly uncomfortable.

'I am sorry for being late. For how long have you been waiting?' she asked quickly settling down.

'About half an hour. The bus ride did not take as long as I had expected.' He smiled.

'You took a bus?' She asked absentmindedly and then immediately cursed herself.

He didn't seem to pay attention to her remark. 'Happy birthday Chhavi ji ... sorry Chhavi,' he said.

'Thank you so much for coming over. Let's order some lunch first. I am famished,' she said.

The waiter kept two glasses of water on the table and waited for the order.

'What will you have Krishna?' she asked glancing at the menu. He went through the names of a few dishes; they looked alien.

'I am not sure. My knowledge of Chinese food is just limited to Chowmein,' he said as a matter of fact.

'Ok, then let's order some chilli chicken, honey potato, chicken Lollypop along with steamed rice and egg noodles. You do eat non vegetarian, I hope?' she asked. He nodded.

'How come you eat non-vegetarian food despite being a Brahmin?' He was visibly surprised.

'We don't cook non-vegetarian at home, but do eat outside. Everyone eats in the family, even Baba,' she said casually flipping through the menu.

'No Brahmin family in the village does,' he said, resigning to her revelation.

She looked at the waiter, handing him the menu. 'So that will be our order. Please make the chicken a bit spicy,' she said.

'Anything to drink madam?' the waiter asked.

'Two bottles of Coke should be fine,' she said.

'I have a small gift for you. I am not sure whether you will like it,' Krishna said hesitatingly after the waiter had left.

She looked all excited. 'Oh really, Krishna? I love gifts. Show me, show me, show me,' she pleaded. He kept a small box on the table. It was wrapped in a bright red-coloured paper.

She grinned before picking it up and then carefully peeled the paper away. A small brown coloured corrugated box appeared underneath. She looked up and smiled at him again before opening it. A young Lord Krishna bobble head lay inside. She tapped its enlarged head gently and the head started to bobble cutely.

'It's so nice. That's a wonderful gift Krishna. Thank you,' she said and clutched his hand.

'I didn't know what else interests you, so couldn't think of anything better,' he said sounding unsure.

'I love it,' she said engrossed in tapping the head and watching the young Krishna shake his head.

'Where did you get this from?' she asked.

'Near the temple on Gomti Bridge. There is a small shop that sells it,' he said.

'Why do you doubt yourself so much Krishna?' She asked. 'In everything that you do. Be it the poetry that you write or the gift that you buy?

Krishna looked sideways. 'We have sorely missed being appreciated for anything in our lives. Good for nothing fellows who landed up on this earth because God defaulted,' he said tapping Lord Krishna's bobble head. 'Perhaps when it comes to things where others have to judge me, I am tentative.'

Chhavi sipped water from the glass. 'I don't think you need to keep your past as a benchmark for everything that you do in the present. Unless you distance yourself from it, the fear will always stop you from giving your best.'

'It's easier said than done. I have been privy to it since my birth. I can't just wash away my hands from my past,' he said.

'You can't; in fact, no one can. All I want to say is keep distance from it and don't make it your permanent residence,' she said.

The waiter arrived and like a juggler, neatly arranged all the dishes on the table within minutes.

She looked at the array of dishes. 'Can we eat now? The aroma has whetted my appetite.'

Krishna stretched his arm to pick up the bowl of rice but she tapped his hand midway. 'It's my birthday so I am going to be doing everything...which includes serving the food.'

'Do you like it?' she asked biting on the chicken lollypop.

'This is the tastiest food I have ever had,' Krishna said lost in the array of delicacies.

'Can I tell you a story?' she asked with the fork in her mouth.

'Another one from your grandmother's treasure?' he asked.

She smiled, nodding.

In the deep blue waters of the ocean there lived a little fish. She was very pretty and all the other sea creatures envied her. But the fish was very unhappy. All day long she would look at herself in the mirror and look at her tail. 'What an ugly tail do I have while all of my other friends have such pretty tails? Why can't I have a tail like them?' the fish would lament. Feeling unhappy, she decided to pay a visit to the friendliest creature in the sea who was a doctor. The president of sea creatures' association, Uncle Octopus. 'Uncle Octopus, I want to get my tail operated,' the fish said impatiently to the sea creature. Uncle Octopus looked at the fish calmly, 'But why would you want to do this? You have such a beautiful tail.'

The fish said, 'No Uncle, just look at the ugly two ends of my tail; they look like a pair of scissors. Look at my friends having such beautiful tails,' the fish said.

Uncle Octopus said, 'Listen dear, there used to be a time when I happened to be very impatient and short tempered over my form. I thought that my round head resembled a bomb while these eight hands of mine looked like eight ugly snakes.'

The fish was astonished. 'Really Uncle! You must have felt terrible. How come you are so friendly and popular now?' the fish asked.

The octopus smiled and said, 'It was simple dear. I did not run away from my weaknesses, but instead turned them into strengths. I did not cut off my hands but instead I started using them to help others. Obviously with more number of hands than anybody else, I could help others like no one else in the sea could. That is the reason I am known as the friendliest creature and everybody around loves me.'

The fish smiled after a long time. 'But how did you get rid of your anger and impatience, Uncle?'

The octopus said, 'I didn't! I just brought out the positive aspect of my personality. Due to my impatient nature, I started working faster and harder than anybody else and I used my anger to safeguard the rights of weaker sea creatures.'

'But what use is my ugly tail?' the fish asked. 'You will be able to understand this when the right time comes,' the octopus said.

On their way back home, both of them got caught in fishing net. 'Damn! What do we do now?' the worried octopus asked.

'Uncle, I have an idea,' the fish said. 'Let me use my scissor like tail to cut through the net.' Soon with the help of her tail, both of them were set free.

Uncle Octopus smiled and said, 'If it was not for your tail, both us would have been dead. Do you still want to get it operated?'

The fish said confidently, 'No uncle, I truly understand how valuable my tail is. I will never compare myself with others from now. You have taught me to respect myself.'

Chhavi spoke polishing off the last strand of noodle from her plate. 'My grandmother said that each one of us has something bad within that we don't like. It is useless to cry about it all the time for it would worsen the shortcoming and the existing circumstances further. The best thing is to channelize it positively in your personality. The shortcomings will soon turn into your strength.'

'Am I the fish here?' Krishna asked.

'All of us are. The question is do we remain what we are or change quickly to become what we truly can,' Chhavi said smiling warmly.

Krishna was amazed at the simple story and the wisdom it carried. She called for the bill and cleared it.

'Can I drop you somewhere?' she asked standing next to the SUV once out of the restaurant.

'No, I think there is a direct bus from here to the University,' Krishna said. 'Thank you for the meal.'

'Thank you for the lovely gift Krishna. I will always cherish it.'

'And I will remember your story. Always,' he said.

'It's good to hear that you are eating meals with your once-upon-a-time foe so frequently,' Shiv said lying on the cot.

'She wasn't my enemy. It was Gope who wanted to stop her,' Krishna said sitting on the chair.

'Ok, so you have changed your tune now. The companionship of a high caste has changed this Dalit sitting here,' Shiv mocked.

Krishna shook his head in disbelief. 'Nothing has changed. I am merely stating facts,' he said.

'I hope you get other facts right as well, Krishna,' Shiv countered.

'What other facts?' Krishna asked.

'Do not forget who you are. We are not used to mixing up with girls, even more so a girl like Panditji's daughter Chhavi. She is like the morning sun; the closer you go, the faster you will burn,' Shiv said.

'We meet like other normal boys and girls in the University. She likes my company and I like hers. What's wrong with friendship?' Krishna said.

'You and I are not normal Krishna,' Shiv said heatedly.

He paused and took a deep breath. 'You saved her from an accident, and perhaps she feels a lot of gratitude towards you. Don't mistake it for any feeling other than this. You are like a new toy in her cupboard. She will be excited about it for a few days after which it would fade away,' Shiv said.

'Do you tell the toy stories that your grandmother told you?' Krishna asked.

Krishna read the last few lines of the book over and over again, "Love means not ever having to say that you are sorry" before keeping it aside. He had finally read his first English book from start till finish and could grasp it fully. It was difficult for him to fathom how he could do it: was the language too simple, was it his strong will that no matter what he would finish it, or the message so sublime that anybody could grasp it? He kept *Love Story* aside and pulled himself out of bed. He looked at his face in the mirror that desperately needed a shave.

He was wiping off the lather from his face when there was a gentle knock on the door.

'Hi Krishna,' she said standing at the door. Krishna didn't have a cloth on his upper body so he quickly picked up his kurta lying on the bed.

She entered his room. 'Didn't see you in the campus for the last couple of days, so I thought of coming over.'

'I have been having my classes after three, perhaps that's why,' he said and gestured at her to sit on the chair.

She stretched her hand that held a vegetable bag, 'I don't have another class now. I thought we could make some lunch?'

Krishna peeked inside; there were some potatoes and a cauliflower. He kept the bag on the table.

'I just finished the book you gave me.' He smiled.

'That's nice. Did you like it?' she asked.

He nodded. 'It's beautiful. So simple, yet touches your heart!'

'Your writing is no less Krishna. Really,' she said.

'Really?'

She merely smiled.

'I am going back to my village tomorrow... for a few days,' he said. Her face stiffened.

'Baba isn't keeping well. My younger brother had called the hostel last night,' he said.

'He will be fine soon. Don't worry,' she said touching his shoulder.

'How is Panditji?' he asked.

'He came back home after seven days yesterday. Politics isn't an affair for him on the side, but like a full time marital responsibility,' she said.

Krishna put the pressure cooker on the electric stove and poured some water inside.

'I can chop the vegetables,' she said.

Krishna waited for a moment and then passed the knife to her along with an empty plate. She took out the potatoes from the bag and started peeling them.

'My mother passed away when I was an infant and neither of my brothers was old enough to shoulder any responsibility. Three toddlers, alongside a man who had his feet deep down in politics,' she said.

'I can understand. It must have been tough for him,' he said.

She nodded. 'Baba never left us lonely. He has always been there to share our joys and shelter us if any trouble arrived. In fact, he knows much more about the three of us individually than we do about each other.

'God has a strange way of running the world. On the one hand he strikes you with an adversity that knocks you down, while on the other hand he gives you the courage to emerge out of it much stronger. Baba has infused this spirit in all of us.'

'Panditji indeed loves you very much. You wouldn't remember your mother, no?' he asked.

'I was very young when she passed away, but from whatever I have gathered, she was a woman who had a mind of her own. She married Baba in her early twenties and passed away before she had reached her thirtieth year,' she said.

'My nani tells me that when she was with Baba, he took a backseat in running the affairs of the house along with his personal life.'

Krishna sat down on the cot. 'I can see your mother in you,' he said.

She diverted her attention from the vegetables in the plate, 'What do you mean?'

'You are today what your mother was yesterday. One can rely on you as well,' Krishna said.

She smiled warmly. 'Yes, one can.'

'Do you want me to put the vegetables in the rice,' he said stretching his hand out. She handed the plate to him.

'What do you want to do Krishna... after finishing your University course?' she asked.

'I want to go to Mumbai and write there. Books, newspapers and perhaps also for films,' he said a bit hesitatingly.

She said without flinching, 'That seems like a good idea. We have some distant cousins who have been living in Mumbai all their lives. Let me find out if they can give some leads,' she said. Krishna nodded.

'Do you want to read something out?' she asked.

'Yes, something that I wrote last night,' he said taking out his diary.

इंतज़ार अब एक प्रिय आदत सी है
जैसे सर्द सुबह की कंपकपी को गर्म रौशनी की चुस्की का
मीलों चले निढाल राही को शरीर भर बसेरे का
इस पल के निर्मम दु:ख को बस अगले पल के सहारे का
आखिरी सांस लेते मनुष्य को अपने नए जोड़े का
इंतजार का रंग सफ़ेद है, पुनीत
तुम्हारे आने से इसमें रंग भरेगा
कुछ ऐसे कि जैसे बारिश छोड़ जाती है अपने पीछे अनेकों
इंतजार की कोई सीमा भी नहीं है
कुछ हमारे प्यार जैसी या जैसे तुम्हारा सौंदर्य
इसकी कोई खुशबू भी नहीं
वह भरती है तुमसे मिलने के बाद, कुछ ऐसे की अनंत तक दुनिया महके
इस इंतज़ार को आदत बनाना अब मजबूरी सी हो चली है
क्योंकि प्यार हो चला है मुझे अब इस से भी

She sighed deeply. 'How can you write like this about love? Have you ever been in love before?'

He shook his head, 'No, never.'

'Then how can you write so deeply about it without experiencing it?' she asked.

'It's the first time that I have written about love. It was written last night,' he said.

'Recent?' She smiled, a tinge of shyness showing on her face. He nodded.

The pressure cooker whistle interrupted the myriad emotions running across their hearts.

Krishna served the rice in plates and placed a brand new bottle of pickle on the table.

'I got it yesterday, thinking you may like it,' he said gesturing at it.

She grinned looking at him, 'Now that you are pampering me, would you mind opening the cap too?'

Chhavi had finished early as she gazed at Krishna finishing off the last morsel of rice from his plate.

'There are a few grains stuck over your lips,' she pointed out. Krishna rubbed his finger at the wrong place above his mouth.

She stretched her hand to reach his mouth; being unable to, she got up from the chair and sat next to him. 'Wait,' she said before gently plucking away the grains from his skin. It was perhaps destined that in that moment her eyes looking into his would find love glowing inside. She reached out to his lips and kissed them. Krishna sat there unmoved. The sweet dampness over his lips reminded him that he had been loved, but only after she had moved away. They sat there motionless for a while, under the whirring fan.

'Can we go out somewhere?' she asked, her face a tinge redder. Krishna nodded and got up from the cot.

The cycle rickshaw turned left before the Hanuman Temple on University Road and meandered its way through the crowd. Men, women and children crowded shops that sold all kinds of temple paraphernalia required to appeal any devout visitor to the acclaimed temple. The river lay lazily on one side while on the other, houses of varying sizes popped their heads up. It was called the New Hyderabad Colony.

Chhavi asked the rickshaw puller to drop them at one end of the road. The cemented road ran a few feet above the banks of the river and there wasn't much noise.

'Let's walk next to the river,' she said stepping down from the cemented road. Krishna followed her.

The sunlight was dipping amidst a pleasant breeze. Small children wearing frugal clothes played cricket with a torn ball at a distance.

'What do *you* want to do after finishing your studies?' Krishna asked.

'Me?' Chhavi smiled. 'I want to travel the world first and then settle down to teach kids in some village.'

'I wish someone could have taught me back in the village,' Krishna said. 'The roots of your family lie in a village too. It should not be difficult for you to fulfil your desire.'

Chhavi smiled wryly. 'Provided it is in line with what my family expects from me.'

'Panditji comes across as an open-hearted reasonable man. No?' he asked.

She nodded. 'Baba isn't averse to granting freedom, but only within limits. Sometimes the love for our children comes in the way of what our children love. It is a terrible choice to make.'

'Chhavi,' Krishna called out her name instinctively for the first time. She stared at him.

'Can I reciprocate your kiss?' he asked. She nodded gently before coming closer. Krishna held her by the waist and let his lips gently squeeze hers. They parted after a few seconds before coming together again for another kiss and then for one more. Each more passionate than the previous, more loving, more binding.

They were climbing up on the main road when she spoke, 'Krishna, I am coming with you to your village.'

It didn't seem to surprise him much. 'Will Panditji agree?' She shook her head, negative.

'I will manage somehow,' she said signalling at a rickshaw to stop.

'Aren't you coming?' she said. The cycle rickshaw waited ahead.

'I will walk to the hostel. You will have to take a detour to drop me,' he said.

'What time is the train tomorrow?' she asked.

'6 in the evening. Avadh Assam Express,' he said.

'I will meet you at the ticket window on the station. Does 5.00 p.m. sound ok?' she said. He nodded.

'Krishna,' she paused to hold his hand. 'There are two people in my life who I love the most. The first is my father and the second is you now. I want you to know this.'

She left him behind, shrouded under the warmth of her words, the fragrance of her body and the tenderness of her touch.

The train chugged its way out of the Charbagh railway station, half an hour late. They sat facing each other in the sleeper coach amongst people.

'I have told Baba that we have a department educational trip near Patna for which presence is mandatory,' she said adjusting her dupatta.

'Didn't he ask for a contact number?' Krishna asked.

'It's a short trip. I have told him that once I reach, I will call him to give details. We will give a number that is close to your house,' she said excited about her escapade.

'We don't have tickets for the sleeper coach. I usually travel in the general compartment,' he said.

She flashed out two general tickets, 'That's why we have bought these. The upgrade, I think, we will manage. I have seen my brothers doing this all the time when we are travelling.'

He smiled doubtfully. 'Fine, but why did you decide to come? The stay in my village is not going to comfort you. You aren't used to a life like that.'

She smiled warmly. 'I would any day prefer body discomfort to an anxious heart. I would have missed you Krishna. It was better that I come along.'

'Ticket, ticket,' the Ticket Collector stretched his hand in front of Krishna. Chhavi pulled out the tickets from her purse and placed them in his hand.

The middle aged TC looked over his thick glasses resting on his broad nose, 'Madam, this isn't the compartment where you should be sitting. You require a reservation here.'

'Shuklaji, a Brahmin not keen to help another belonging to his clan is a huge sin,' she said gazing at the badge hanging loosely on his black coat.

The TC looked at his badge once, that said 'Ramakant Shukla' and then at Chhavi – 'Everyone becomes a Brahmin here if they don't have a ticket or want to be upgraded.'

Chhavi took out her identity card and flashed it in front of his eyes, 'Shuklaji, I won't lie for such a small favour. It's just that a few of us are going for an educational trip near Patna, all my friends have got confirmed berths, except the two of us.'

The TC nodded, 'Unfortunately, there is more required to run a house than just helping your own breed,' he said with a mischievous smile.

Chhavi could sense what he hinted at. 'If this was Lucknow, I wouldn't have had to repeat my request Shuklaji,' she said firmly.

The TC was taken in by her confidence. 'Where do you belong?'

'I am Panditji's daughter,' she said.

The TC thought for a few seconds, 'Panditji? Who exactly are you referring to?'

'Pandit Radhey Shankar Mishra,' she said. The expression on the TC's face changed in an instant as he looked at her ID card.

'Are you Panditji's daughter? Why didn't you tell me before?' he said all shaken up.

'I was trying to, but...'

Chhavi was interrupted by the TC. 'You are like my daughter, why wouldn't I help you? Take berth number 26 and 27; I am confirming them in your name.'

'Thank you Shuklaji. Do I need to give you some money?' she asked opening her bag.

The TC pushed it aside. 'Not at all. Can a father take money from his daughter? You only tell me?' he asked. Chhavi shook her head in the negative. He shifted his gaze from her towards other passengers and checked their tickets.

He got up to leave after he had finished. 'Give my regards to Panditji, and if ever you need help on this train, remember that your Uncle Ramakant Shukla is always there.'

Krishna looked at her with admiration along with other co-passengers who were awestruck.

'Panditji wields enough clout in and around Lucknow,' he said after the TC had left.

'Yes, when the Brahmin card didn't seem to work, I knew his name would,' she said.

They got down at the Darbhanga station around noon. The train was delayed by a couple of hours.

'I hope we get a bus to the village soon. The connectivity isn't good in this area,' he said.

The platform bustled with people; the air was humid and smelly. Krishna walked ahead of her, turning back after every few moments to confirm her presence. The district bus depot was close to the station but the approach road to it was a disaster. There were piles of sludge stuck on the ground and with filth running over it from the neighbouring drains, the road was a real nightmare to walk. The buses were lined up one after the other and as they left the depot, a lot of the wet muck would fly around, disturbed abruptly by the heavy wheels of the bus.

'You won't be able to walk here. I told you coming here wasn't a good idea,' Krishna said helplessly.

She had her face covered with a dupatta; only her eyes could be seen. 'I will wait here. Why don't you go and look for tickets?' she said. He looked into her eyes, they were confident enough.

He came back with the tickets after half an hour where she waited with a water bottle in her hand. She had kept her hand luggage on a cart that was placed behind. It sold drinking water, each glass for a rupee. People stood there next to it, drinking water and stealing glances at her.

'We were lucky. The bus leaves in ten minutes,' he said and signalled at the bus standing third in the row. She smiled and held his hand as they walked through the wet muck, looking for dry patches, taking measured steps.

"We should be there in a couple of hours,' he said as the bus moved out of the Darbhanga bus depot. The humidity and smell of diesel filled their nostrils.

'It's fine. You want water?' she passed him the bottle. He opened the cap and gulped some.

'You won't find this at home. We drink water from the hand pump,' he said raising the bottle.

'I have stayed in a village before…Baba's native village. It's near Sitapur,' she said looking away.

'Your world is very different than mine. You will see it for yourself,' he said.

A row of roadside eateries appeared all of a sudden, 'Why do all of them have "Line Hotel" attached to their names?' she asked looking at the glow signs hanging over them.

'It's the local equivalent for "dhaba". There is one major difference though; most of these serve non-vegetarian fare, unlike north. There seems to be more fondness for meat and liquor here,' he replied.

The bus had hit the highway and was picking up speed. Krishna looked at her; she looked out of the window, at the green patches of land that lined up the countryside, ponds, animals walking in the fields and on the nearby muddy lanes. Suddenly he felt soothing warmness oozing out from his heart. Krishna smiled to himself; *he was going home with her.*

'We are almost there,' Krishna said as the bus took a U turn from the highway to enter a narrow road. The plaque read 'MANIGACHHI' written in charcoal ink. He looked at Chhavi; she had dozed off as the pleasant breeze left every tired body comforted. A loose strand of hair flapped on her cheek; he picked it up and carefully rested it behind her ear. She opened her eyes to smile at Krishna, her eyes drowsy. "Have we reached your village?'

Krishna nodded, 'That's the nearest station to our village. There is a train from here that takes you twice every day to Darbangha.'

She looked at the lonely station; a couple of shops outside sold samosas and sweets that looked lifeless. The bus sashayed on the dusty road moving swiftly over the patches of concrete and cobblestones. It passed through a vast green expanse with paddy fields taking most of the land on both sides, occasionally a few acres of wheat crop would become visible and then a little crop of pulse would spring out from here and there.

'What's that?' she pointed at a man made pond with high boundary walls.

'They use it for breeding fish. It belongs to Yadavs; my father works in fields they own,' he said.

The bus halted after a couple of kilometres. They got down on a stone-laden rough pathway. 'We will have to walk two kilometres from here to reach my house,' he said.

The lane going into the village looked desolate; a bunch of old men clad just in their vests stopped their chatter to stare at them as they passed. An old woman sat in the courtyard pouring her little left energy into the grinding bowl. She looked distracted to see them, muttered something to herself, and then got back to her task. The stray dogs looked attentive with their presence, sniffed the air, and rested their heads back on the ground.

'Why is it so quiet at this time?' she asked.

'They sleep in the afternoon, if there isn't too much work to do in the fields,' he said.

A few young boys who looked like students stood near a small tea shop ahead. They stared at them for a while and then muttered something amongst themselves. She could hear a chuckle.

'Do they know you?' she asked after they had passed them. He nodded.

'Why didn't they greet you then?' she asked.

'They all belong to the family of Yadavs. They don't acknowledge people who work for them. They are not considered to be equals,' he said.

They stopped after walking for another five minutes. Krishna gazed around.

'What we have left behind is where the high castes live. This is where our land begins,' he said.

Chhavi could spot the difference quite distinctly between the two divided domains. The houses on this side were worn out, holding themselves on the dry land. The open drains carried filth and an overpowering stench that seemed to suffuse the air. Chhavi covered her face once again, forcing herself not to vomit. The men looked weak, stomachs touching their back, squatting on the floor or some on the cot in their verandah; the walls were adorned with *uplas,* i.e. dung cakes. The women hid behind thatched walls of a small room that looked like a kitchen, peeping out occasionally from under their veils. Their eyes smelt of curiosity and their gaze carried a tacit coldness.

Krishna stopped in front of a house that looked as decrepit as others and gestured at her to walk inside. The boundary wall of the house was made of hardened mud that had cracked up at various places, making it uneven.

In front of the door hung a brown coloured sack that doubled up as a curtain and the door itself. He asked Chhavi to wait at the door and entered the house. She could hear the sound of a man coughing profusely and mumbling something to Krishna; it seemed like his father. A woman had started crying suddenly; it was his mother. Krishna was calming them down, asking them about their well-being, telling them about his life in the unknown city. He came out with his mother in a few minutes.

'Who is she?' she asked startlingly, covering her head with the loose end of the sari. His mother was taller than Chhavi had expected a woman in the village would be, her hair oiled and combed back, a soft face lined with perched wrinkles.

'She is the sister of a close friend in the University,' Krishna said. His father came out limping and looking equally perplexed. Their son standing with an unknown woman in front of them wasn't an everyday sight.

'Why has she come here?' his mother asked.

'Amma, she is doing a project. Researching different kind of soils in the village fields,' he could only think of this excuse at the moment.

The father who wore only a vest above his crumpled dhoti looked up, 'Project? What is that?'

Krishna shook his head. 'You won't understand, Bau. If you don't complete this, the University doesn't let you pass.'

The father nodded, 'Ohh!' with profound seriousness.

'Is she going to stay here?' his mother asked. Krishna nodded. 'But there is no space Krishna,' his mother said. Chhavi was rooted with embarrassment.

'It's a question of two days. We can manage,' he said.

'You are here only for two days? Is it?' His mother's eyes dampened again.

'I am here only to see Bau. I have my exams in a month,' he said.

'What caste does she belong to?' his mother asked.

Krishna hesitated for a moment. 'She is a Brahmin.' His words evoked no response from the parents, as if that had numbed them.

'Brahmin?' His mother shrieked as if a live goddess was standing in front of her. In an instant she bowed down attempting to touch Chhavi's feet. Chhavi jumped back or else his mother would have been successful.

Krishna held her by the arm. 'Amma, don't do that. They don't believe in discrimination anymore in big cities,' he lied.

Krishna's father who had moved a couple of steps back spoke with all the energy left, 'You want a Brahmin girl to stay in our house, eat with us, breathe the air that we do... all twenty-four hours. This will be a sin that can't be undone.'

'Bau, it's fine,' she addressed his father the way Krishna had. 'No one in my family back in Lucknow believes in all of this. Krishna has eaten in my house in Lucknow; we don't even think like this.'

The father raised his eyebrow to gaze at Krishna. 'Have you gone there to study or eat tasty food at the house of Brahmins?'

'I have just eaten there once, Bau,' Krishna replied. 'Amma, it's just a matter of two days. Please let her stay.'

'What if others in the village ask?' she said looking at her husband.

'Two days Amma; by the time they realize, we will be gone. If they do, tell them she is the sister of a Dalit friend of mine from Lucknow.' He looked at Chhavi who didn't seem to mind at being called a low caste. She nodded.

'She can't pass off as a Dalit girl, Krishna. Her skin glows like fresh milk and there is happiness that I see in her eyes. None of us have it,' she said. The realization made everyone go quiet.

She glanced at Chhavi. 'You would be tired after a long journey. I will fetch some water for you to take a bath. Krishna, why don't you keep her bag inside?'

Chhavi entered the room, overwhelmed with its size and simplicity. Old calendars with pictures of different deities were stuck in one corner, two garlanded small statues of Lord Ganesh and Goddess Lakshmi – responsible for prosperity and happiness in the house – stood atop a small cotton cloth. Half-burnt incense sticks were dangling behind calendars, raising their heads in different directions. The remaining space in the room jostled with many other items; a multitude of bundles of clothes, a cot on which

Krishna's father slept, a mat for his mother and younger brother, an aluminium suitcase that had a lock on it, housing the family's valuables. It was difficult for her to imagine that the man she loved now had spent most of his life in the same tiny room fighting for space with a million other things.

Krishna kept her bag over the aluminium suitcase. 'So, that's my home,' he said.

'Home is where your heart is. The size of it really doesn't matter,' she said. He nodded. She took out her towel from the bag.

'You will need to take a fresh pair of clothes as well,' he said. She looked curious.

'Amma will stand guard with a cloth near the hand-pump. There isn't a separate toilet here and you will need to bathe with your clothes on,' he said.

What he said gave her goose bumps. 'You have to bathe in open? What if someone is watching?' she said nervously.

'No one can. The hand pump is in one corner behind Gauri's shed. The view is blocked from three sides and *Amma* will be standing in front,' he said.

'But then, one needs to change after taking a bath,' she said, the apprehension not wearing away.

'Don't worry, once you take a bath there, you will be confident enough to change clothes,' he said with a half-smile.

She punched him on the shoulder. 'How cruel can you be, Krishna?' and left the room.

Krishna sat in the verandah talking to his father when she walked back after a bath. Her soft skin glowed after being cleansed; his mother was right, she couldn't pass off as one amongst them. His mother walked behind.

'It was the first time for her. She was a bit scared,' his mother said. 'It will be fine from tomorrow.' His father looked the other way.

'Give me some time to get lunch ready,' she said. 'Why don't you go and take a bath Krishna?'

Chhavi talked to his mother squatting on the floor outside their kitchen made of mud. It was dark inside and despite the afternoon sun, only his mother's face was visible behind the flames that stemmed from the chulha. She could see wood, pieces of charcoal and dung cakes inside it, providing fuel to the burning fire.

'Where is Krishna's brother? Don't see him around,' she asked.

His mother looked her way, 'Ganesh? He is in school, should be back any moment.'

'Amma, can I help?' she asked.

'Don't bother. A Brahmin eating with us is in itself a crime; on top of it if you help me in cooking... I can't imagine how much more sin we will accumulate. Not at all,' she said touching both her ears.

Krishna had bathed and peeked inside the kitchen. 'Amma, is the food ready? The hunger is killing.'

'Go and take out two plates from the suitcase. I am laying the food outside,' she said. Krishna nodded and walked inside, Chhavi followed him.

He took the key kept under the mat, removed Chhavi's bag and unlocked the suitcase under it. She didn't look inside. He took out two glass plates and locked the suitcase again.

'Why only two? There are more who will eat,' she said.

'They are only for you and me. If you were not my guest, I wouldn't get this privilege either,' he said.

'But Krishna...,' she tried to resist.

'It comes to us naturally, Chhavi. She has been doing this all her life. If you force her to do something else, that will be unnatural. Come!' he pulled her hand.

The food was laid out; one vegetable, rice, rotis and a dal. It had the inherent latent flavour of food picked directly from the soil; unadulterated. They sat on a mat laid in the verandah. The food was put in open bowls. It attracted a lot of flies. His father, who ate with them, saw her discomforted and got up. He picked up a straw hand fan and started waving it over her to ward off the flies. She was aghast and stopped eating.

'Please sit down and eat. You can't be doing this,' she tried to stop him. The old man didn't pay attention but continued doing what he was.

'Bau, leave it, she will manage,' Krishna said.

He looked at his son annoyingly. 'You eat quietly. Let me do what I am supposed to.'

Chhavi wanted to resist further but he gestured at her to relax. 'What did I tell you inside? Please do as I say here,' he muttered. She went quiet, and began eating.

A young boy with big eyes walked in; he was wearing grey half-pants, and a crumpled white shirt with threads hanging out of the collar.

'Bhaiya, when did you come?' he said gleefully.

His mother replied, 'He came a while ago. Sit down and eat Ganesh.'

He touched Krishna's feet and then glanced at Chhavi. 'Who is she?' he asked reluctantly.

'She is the sister of bhaiya's close friend. Touch her feet as well,' Krishna's father intervened waving the fan.

He looked at her and then bowed down. She smiled, touching his hair.

'Now, let me show you a place that you will love,' Krishna said looking at her. It had been an hour that they had finished lunch. Ganesh sat in the verandah reading from his school book. His father slept on the cot inside and mother was in the cow-shed feeding the buffalo, Gauri.

They walked behind the house on a narrow lane for a couple of minutes before their view opened up suddenly. A majestic banyan tree stood with aplomb, lush green; and behind it a pond that sparkled with water. Hundreds of species of birds sat over the tree, chirping, as it stretched open its arms to shelter each one. The warm greenery around the pond along with the passionate shade the tree lent robbed the sunlight of its leftover sheen. What remained were serenity, solitude, and bliss.

'It's beautiful Krishna,' Chhavi said holding his hand. A small baby-goat was tied to one of the branches of the tree and looked intimidated by their presence.

'All that you see here,' he said pointing at the tree and the pond, 'belongs to all of us, living in this part of the village. A few years back, all the women folk used to bathe here but we stopped that after learning from upper castes that the pond can make money for us. Now we also breed fish here for which everyone contributes and the fish belong to everybody.'

'I wish time could just stop ticking and I stay trapped in this moment, here,' she said mesmerized.

'The nights and early mornings are even better. We can come again,' he said. She gazed at him and clutched his hand even tighter.

The night arrived early in the village. The light from the lantern was sufficient for the verandah but couldn't travel further beyond, a couple of feet in the courtyard. Krishna sat with Ganesh clarifying his doubts in arithmetic. Chhavi stared at the silence resting within the thick blanket of darkness, waking up abruptly to the sound of crickets. His parents had retired for the night; mother had to start work at four next morning in the cowsheds of Yadavs and his father to start the battle with his illness, afresh.

'Let's go and sit by the pond,' he said tapping her shoulder. She looked up to see his face and nodded.

'Bhaiya, can I come too?' Ganesh asked hesitatingly.

'Why not Ganesh,' she said holding his hand.

The three of them sat under the tree, gazing at the pond, watching the ripples playing gently with the moonlight that fell over them.

'What do you want to become when you grow up Ganesh?' Chhavi asked.

'Me?' The young boy's face drew a blank. 'I don't know. I will become whatever bhaiya, Bau and Amma want me to,' he said.

'I didn't ask you about others' opinion, of what they want you to be. What do you want?' she asked.

The question made him nervous. 'Bau wants me to join the army. Amma wants me to become a doctor,' he said.

'And what does bhaiya want?' she glanced at Krishna.

'He says, first complete your studies,' Ganesh said. She put her hand on his head tenderly.

'Everyone has an opinion and loves giving one. Some may want you to do things in one way while others may want you to try a different thing. But unless you like doing either, the chance is, that you will fail. So it's important to listen to others, especially your family because they love you, but in the end you should do what you really want to,' she said stroking his hair.

'Do you understand Ganesh?'

The young boy stared at her for a moment and then nodded. His affirmation looked unconvincing.

Chhavi sensed his hesitation and paused. 'Let me tell you a short story. Ok?' The young boy nodded, this time more convincingly.

Krishna reclined on the grass. 'She has a million stories in her head, Ganesh. Humour her and she will tell you many.'

She smiled and punched him on the leg.

One day a father and son were taking their donkey to the market to sell it. They met with a person who was travelling in the opposite direction. 'Ha ha. How silly! Why didn't one of you think of riding your donkey instead of walking?' He laughed.

So the man put his son on the donkey and they continued their journey. Soon they came across another group of men. One of them told the boy, 'How disrespectful this is, lazy fellow! How can you let your poor father walk, while you ride the donkey?'

So the man took his son off and climbed on the donkey himself. After walking for a while they met two women who shouted at them. 'What kind of a father are you? The poor boy is walking in this heat and so much of dust while you are enjoying your ride.'

So the man pulled his son up on the donkey as well and they rode together. After a few hours they reached a bridge, after crossing which they would enter the town. They met a couple there, who admonished them, 'Just because the donkey is born to take care of man's burden, it doesn't mean that you overload it with excess weight of you both.'

Listening to them, both the father and son got down from the donkey. They tied the donkey's legs upside down to a pole and shouldered each end of the pole. They started crossing the bridge carrying the donkey on their shoulders. The donkey was scared and started kicking fiercely. The father and son couldn't maintain their balance and the pole slipped from their hands and fell into the river along with the donkey. The strong current in the river swept the donkey away and the father and son were left with nothing.

Chhavi took a long deep breath and looked at the young boy. Ganesh looked at her and said, 'Listening to others too often may harm you. If the father and son would have taken their own decisions, they would have reached the town and sold off the donkey as well.'

'Very good Ganesh, and that is why when you have to take important decisions in your life, listen to others, but to your heart the most,' she said patting his back.

Krishna felt the stillness around, the smell of damp earth over which they sat, glistening water in the pond and then gazed at her patting his brother's back gently. His life, like the night of today, had never been prettier.

They sat at the edge of a paddy field, under a tree, early in the day. They were resting their back on the tree trunk.

'Life seems to go in a slow motion here,' she said looking at him. He nodded his head.

'I feel like kissing you,' she said.

'Don't even dare. Can't you see so many people working in the fields?' Krishna glanced anxiously at the scores of men bending down in the fields; their tanned bare backs facing the sun.

Chhavi whispered, 'They are too busy working hard,' and moved closer to Krishna's face.

He moved away. 'Can I ask you something?' he said. She looked at him.

'Do you think we have a future?'

'Krishna, do you love me?' she asked.

He nodded. 'I have never loved anyone as much, before.'

'Then, what do you worry about?' she asked.

He stared at her. 'I worry about our future, your family's willingness to accept this.'

'You and I don't know what the future looks like. What we have, is just this... the present,' she said.

She glanced back at the open village field. 'Each moment that you and I live in the present should be fulfilling, regardless of what lies in future.'

He turned to look at her. 'I want to be with you. All my life.'

'Like now, Krishna, you always will be,' she said.

The labourers in the field had taken a short break from work. They huddled together at the field's edge drinking water.

'Have you heard of internet Krishna?' she asked.

'Yes, I have read about it. Your message can reach someone sitting anywhere in a matter of seconds on the computer.'

Chhavi smiled. 'Yes, it connects the world. I will open an account for you on Hotmail where I can write to you.'

'Why would you need to write letters when we are together?' he said.

'When you go to Mumbai, stupid,' she said shaking her head.

'Oh! It will take a while before I go there,' he said.

They walked towards the local market. The day was just left with a couple of hours before the evening knocked.

'Why is this market called Bajitpur and not Jalegar? It's hardly a mile away from where you stay,' she asked.

'All these villages – Jalegar, Bajitpur and other neighbouring ones – fall under Manigachi, where the railway station was. It's like the hub of villages; the Railway and Police Station, State Bank are all based there,' he said.

The market was more colourful and noisy than she had thought. The cemented narrow road ran in between a series of shops lined on both the sides. They sold clothes for children and men, saris, groceries and pulses, medicines, jewellery, undergarments, etc., sub-lanes running deeper inside, after every few shops.

'What's inside these lanes? She asked.

'More shops, like these, where you save more,' he said glancing around.

Shops that sold tea and sweets lay scattered in the market. The confectioners were busy in making fresh samosas and jalebis in some, while in other lesser populated ones, lazily chatted with the tea sipping customers.

'What's that?' she pointed at one of the counters.

Krishna looked in her direction. 'Those brown coloured oval balls?' She nodded.

'That's Litti, made out of wheat and lentil; similar to the *kachauri* they make in Lucknow,' he said.

He signalled at the seller for two. They came along with green chutney and onions.

'It is spicy but very tasty,' she said taking a bite. 'Can we have six more of these?' she asked the seller. He packed them all in a newspaper and handed it to Krishna.

'We will take them home,' she said while paying.

They walked ahead in the market. Krishna stopped in front of a shop with iron grills and a small counter.

'What does this shop sell?

Krishna hesitated. 'Toddy. You don't get this in Lucknow. If you don't mind, can I pick up some?'

'Why will I? If that is so good, I would like to try it too,' she said. Just then she spotted a phone booth ahead.

'Krishna,' she called out. He turned around. 'I am going to call Baba,' she pointed at the STD booth. He nodded.

Once home, they sat on the raised platform of the verandah. The night was still as the village prepared for a break before the morning labour. Krishna sipped from the bottle of toddy.

'What is this made of?' Chhavi asked out of curiosity.

'It's fresh sap from the palm tree.'

'Can I take a sip?' she stretched her hand. He handed the bottle to her.

'It smells pungent,' she made a face and then took a sip and then another.

He nodded. 'Locals here love it. It sells cheap and doesn't intoxicate you as much. By the way, did you speak to Panditji?'

'Yes, told him that I will be back the day after.'

'We have a train in the afternoon.'

'It's going to be my last night in your village. I will miss it.'

'You can always return whenever you want to.'

'Yes, I know. Have the others slept?'

'Yes, it's been an hour that we finished eating.'

'I had spoken to others about you helping CSWI. They had their doubts but later they were fine.'

She looked at him, 'The elections are approaching. We need to raise our final issue; the *chautha savaal* (the fourth question). It has to be solid.'

'Yes, it has to be,' he said.

He took a sip of toddy and paused. 'Why didn't you ever ask me the reason why I opposed you in the campus?'

'Because I knew what the reason was. You were misguided and wanted to be in the good books of those who mattered in the campus,' she said.

'You could have asked me who those people are.'

'That's not more important for me than you coming out of their sway,' she said.

'They had planned to scare you by throwing fuel over you, but no one knows who started the fire... not even them,' he said sipping hurriedly.

'Why did you risk yourself for saving me, Krishna?'

She could see tears welling up in his eyes for the first time. 'I was angry with them and foremost with myself for being a part of it. There was no other way I could seek self-redemption,' he said pressing his palms against his eyes.

'So you decided to risk your life,' she said. She pulled him closer and rested his head on her bosom.

'This wasn't a coincidence Krishna. It was destined.' She felt his tears on her shirt, penetrating inside to touch her heart. They sat entwined for a long time.

'Can we go to the pond?' she broke the silence.

Krishna looked up at her. 'Yes. Let's go.'

'Can you take the cot along, for us to sit there?' she asked. He shouldered it and walked behind her. The pond rested in its natural charm. Krishna kept the cot on the ground and they sat down.

She looked at his face; the tears had dried up, leaving white stray marks under his eyes. She kissed him on the lips and then gently licked off the marks from his skin. He kissed her back, hesitation soon turning into a will to possess her.

'Help me get rid of my clothes,' she whispered raising her hands. He took off her long shirt as she slipped the straps of her bra over her arms. He fumbled with the strap of the bra for a while to no avail, which amused her.

'Is that too complicated?' She taunted; it tested him further, and he lunged at it again with desperation, finally unclipping it. He touched her nakedness as she lay down on the bed. He removed his shirt to rest by her side. He kissed her on the lips, on her chest, on the navel and all across her being. Their bodies tangled as they kissed, exploring more of each other. Soon any piece of clothing became a deterrent to their heart's desire. In that momentarily created world, where only the two of them lived, they discovered their unique rhythm of love, following which they travelled all the way to ecstasy. She moaned, looking into his eyes, not knowing that he was vocal, but what his spontaneous utterances brought out was the purity residing in his heart. As they knotted finally to fall together magnificently, nothing else mattered but togetherness.

It's tough to say goodbye to loved ones. The sheer inability to do anything makes you cringe. His mother wept with her head on his shoulders, his father consoling her. Ganesh stood there holding his brother's hand. With sad eyes he asked, 'When will you be back?'

'Very soon,' Chhavi said handing some money to Ganesh. Krishna gestured her not to; she chose to defy him. His mother looked at the small bundle of currency in Ganesh's hand, but did not object. Money was scarce and it wasn't prudent to deny it in any form.

'Hope you were able to finish your project,' his father said.

'I could, Bau. Thank you for accommodating me, despite the discomfort.'

He stretched his hand towards her forehead, not touching it. 'A Goddess stayed here. It's our good fortune. And his,' he glanced at Krishna.

The train galloped through the darkness, blowing its horn intermittently. They sat on the opposite berths looking away through the window pane.

'I miss your village Krishna, very much,' she reminisced.

He shifted his gaze. 'You have just spent two days there. You will soon forget.'

'Krishna,' her eyes pained, 'these two days are enough to last me a lifetime.'

The CSWI meeting was in progress inside the science canteen. Krishna sat next to Chhavi who faced Ravi sitting on the opposite bench. Three other students from the core committee sat with them.

Ravi cleared his throat, 'We need to have our next forum with the students very soon. Others are gaining momentum.'

Chhavi nodded. 'What issue should we be picking up now? We have already raised the key ones – unlawful possession of hostels, unfair use of sports funds and fake admissions under quota.'

'It has to be the one that is most potent,' Krishna said.

Ravi looked up and said, 'It's still difficult for me to believe that one guy who I wouldn't want anywhere close to any of our meetings is sitting and discussing the next issue with me here.'

'People and opinions can change with time,' Krishna said.

Chhavi intervened, 'Guys, we are here to ponder on the issue that we want to be highlighted. Let's focus.'

Ravi gathered himself, 'Yes correct. Let's see if Krishna has any suggestions? As Chhavi says, he has the pulse of the students and a very creative mind,' he said rather condescendingly.

'I do,' Krishna paused. Everybody in the group had their attention and eyes over him.

'I will be the final question,' he said.

'You! The question? What does that mean, Krishna?' she said.

'The University leaders may be crooks, but what gives them the power to bulldoze the system and do as they wish is the support of the students, gullible ones like you and me.'

'So? What's the plan?' Ravi asked hastily.

'Students know that I have opposed CSWI in the past, disrupted their rallies. They have seen me doing that.'

'Yes they do, but then what?' she asked.

'I will stand in front of them to say that I was wrong; naive enough to fall in their trap. I will accept that I was a pawn and they should not become one like me,' he said. Silence fell in between them, for a few minutes.

Chhavi put her hand over his. 'It's a very powerful statement to make. It will reveal the ugly face of University politics. No, Ravi?'

Ravi was still chewing on to Krishna's words.

'I agree that the idea is solid. But I have two questions. First, what if the students ask Krishna to expose the ones who influenced him, and second, these guys are dangerous. Once this happens, you may have to face consequences.'

Krishna took a sip of water from the glass and glanced at Ravi.

'I won't give away the names. That is not important. What is more important is to accept that I was wrong, in front of everybody,' Krishna said and looked at her.

Ravi nodded. 'What about the second question?'

Krishna said thoughtfully, 'If I am not giving away any names, I don't think they have a reason to retaliate.'

'Krishna, such elements are most concerned about losing their grip over the students. If I was one of them, it would rattle me immensely,' Ravi said.

'If we have to unseat them, this seems to be the best bet. I have made up my mind,' he said looking at everybody.

'Sure?' Chhavi asked. He smiled with steely determination.

'Why are you going home so early?' he asked, leaving her at the University gate. 'We could have gone to the hostel.'

'And do what?' she asked wickedly. Her instant response was enough to fluster him.

'Nothing,' he shook his head nervously, getting caught. She laughed.

'I am a good girl, Mr. Krishna Kumar. My grandmother has told me not to visit a young and attractive man's room alone,' she looked around and pulled his cheek lovingly.

'You and your grandmother have taken over my life.' He chuckled.

Her heart warmed up seeing him happy, consistently, for a while.

'Do you regret it?' she asked with mock anger getting into an auto. He smiled and shook his head.

There was a significant crowd in front of the arts department. September was ending; weather was at the cusp of change, heat slowly melting away. Students were scattered in groups, chatting excitedly, some sitting on the stairs.

The CSWI team waited in one corner along with Krishna; today was the day. Ravi looked at his watch. 'Where is Chhavi? She is usually the first one to arrive before a meeting.'

'Did you call her house?' A comrade asked.

Ravi nodded, 'I did, but no one picked up.'

Krishna felt a pang of nervousness travelling up his heart. He rubbed both his palms together.

'There she comes!' Ravi exclaimed, waving at her. Her face looked dry; something was not right.

Krishna walked towards her. 'What is the matter?'

'Baba hasn't been feeling well since he came home last night. He hasn't spoken with anyone in the house,' she said hastily, her face glum.

Ravi and others joined them. 'You can go back and take care of him. We all are here... we will manage,' Krishna said glancing at others. They nodded.

'It's the last meeting that CSWI has. After this I am out of University politics anyway,' she looked persuasively at Krishna.

'Ok, as you say.'

They formed a semicircle facing the Department of Arts; Krishna was standing in the centre. The students looked at them curiously, a few pointed at Krishna and then showing surprise, whispered to each other.

Krishna brought the microphone closer to his mouth. 'Warm Greetings to you my fellow students and friends, from CSWI – the only party in the campus that thinks of student welfare and betterment.' The murmurs got louder as it became certain that Krishna on that day was the voice of CSWI.

A plump girl from the crowd raised her voice. 'You were against all the issues that CSWI had raised in the previous meetings. How come you speak for them today?'

'You ask a question that is valid. Everyone who has been to a CSWI meeting before, knows that,' Krishna paused.

'How can someone who was a protester yesterday become a supporter today?' Krishna said pointing at the CSWI placard. 'Isn't this in itself a huge question? We are raising this issue as our final question or the *chautha savaal* today.

'I protested against CSWI because I was naive and was pushed to do so. The negative anti-student forces here didn't want CSWI to capture your minds and your hearts.'

'Who pushed you to do that?' an elderly student asked.

'That's not so important. What is more relevant is the keenness of such elements who force us into this; and our gullibility to carry their orders.'

'Why did you do it then?' the same student asked.

'I wanted to be in their good books. I wanted favours from them. The same reason why everyone wants to support them – for power, money and fame.'

'How did you turn into a CSWI supporter then?' another student asked.

'I changed because I heard my inner voice. If I wouldn't have, I would also be walking the same path as many others who are out there supporting these leaders.' Krishna looked at Chhavi fleetingly; she was listening to him in rapt attention, her face still worn out.

'The question here is, what do we do now? Do we let this campus be run the way it is, same people coming and ruling this campus year after year? Or do we have the guts to say enough is enough?'

A group of students standing in front shouted with enthusiasm, 'No we can't let this happen; this needs to change now.'

Krishna could see the rising euphoria amongst the students.

He raised his pitch, 'The only way we can bring about a change is by choosing a party that is made up of likeminded students and has the well being of every student in its heart.'

He took out his diary from the bag and started reading from it.

परेशान हूँ पर निराश नहीं, आज हारा हूँ पर हताश नहीं
चोटें खाई हैं पर कमज़ोर नहीं, कुछ पल डरा हूँ पर डरपोक नहीं
सब कुछ खोया है पर कंगाल नहीं, ठोकर खाया हूँ पर अपंग नहीं
तानें सहें हैं पर मायूस नहीं, कुछ पल टूटा हूँ पर बेबस नहीं
सब कुछ सीखा है, कि कुछ अब अनजान नहीं
इतना झेला है कि अब निर्बल नहीं
उस हर वो पल जब मैंने कुछ खोया, तब तब मैंने खुद में कुछ पाया
इस खुद से कुछ खोने ने ही आज मुझे क्या से क्या बनाया

The crowd was pushed into silence once he had finished, the message of hope passionately resonating with them. After few moments of ensuing quietness, the atmosphere reverberated with chants of "Long Live CSWI" that didn't seem to subside for quite some time.

'You nailed it Krishna,' Ravi patted his back breathlessly, 'didn't he?' Chhavi nodded and hugged him unexpectedly. The CSWI team looked surprised with her sudden expression.

She realized her action wasn't appropriate for the moment and separated. 'I was overwhelmed with your speech and the last few lines, that all is not lost as yet. The hope still lives.'

Ravi looked sombre. 'We have to thank you Chhavi, for introducing Krishna to CSWI, or else we wouldn't have ever been privy to what he was capable of.'

'I am not responsible for this,' she said. 'He decided it for himself.'

Ravi's expressions were intact. 'I always thought that guys like him don't have the potential to do anything positive. I was so wrong. Life has taught me a lesson today.' He looked apologetically at Krishna.

'It's not your fault Ravi. Sometime back, I had the same feeling about myself,' Krishna said looking at Chhavi.

Ravi nodded, taking a deep breath. 'You should be leaving Chhavi. We will regroup now and discuss what to do next. I hope Panditji is fine by now.' He walked away with the CSWI group.

'Keep this,' she said handing him a piece of paper. He looked at it; there was a name and a phone number scribbled on it.

'It's my cousin's number and office address in Mumbai. He works for an advertising agency there. Speak to him; he might be of some help.'

Chhavi jumped out of the Tata Safari and climbed up the steps of Vivekananda Hospital hurriedly. The ICU ward was right in front. When she had reached home to a desolate house, she was told that Baba had suffered a heart stroke in the morning. He was admitted in the hospital after he complained of uneasiness, just after she had left for the University.

She was literally running in the corridor when she spotted her grandmother sitting on the bench outside the ICU. Her brothers looked grim, standing near the entrance to the ICU. She sat next to her grandmother, wrapping her shoulders. Her brothers didn't seem to acknowledge her presence.

The old lady looked at Chhavi, her eyes clogged with tears. 'Panditji was talking to Vijay and Anil when he collapsed. There was something wrong with him since yesterday; something that bothered him deeply.'

'Baba will be fine, Nani.' She got up and walked to her elder brother. 'How's he now bhaiya?'

His face hardened looking at her. 'Could you finally find time for the family, from everything else that you have been up to?' She was taken aback by his sharp response, unsure about asking him what he really meant. She went and sat next to her grandmother again.

148

An hour passed. The senior doctor on round entered the ICU and came out after a few minutes.

'Panditji seems to be doing fine. Family members may see him for a few minutes if they wish to,' the doctor told Vijay. He then looked at their Nani and Chhavi sitting on the bench. 'Are they family too?' he asked. Vijay took a deep breath and then nodded.

Baba had never looked like this before. Syringes poked his body, mouth covered with an oxygen mask; he looked frail and dependent. She entered the room in the end and walked to stand behind her grandmother, who sat on the stool near Baba's bed. Her brothers stood opposite, looking anxiously at Baba. He opened his eyes slowly after a while. Baba's gaze travelled from her brother's faces onto his grandmother's and then rested on her. She saw his facial expressions change, from looking pained, she could see a dash of anger on his face.

She held his hand. 'Baba, how are you feeling now?' He pulled his hand away to look the other way.

'Baba, why do you do this? Are you angry with me over something?' she asked looking at his grandmother. Her brothers looked aside. The old lady expressed ignorance. There was silence in the room.

The nurse stood in one corner looking at Baba's test reports. Baba held Vijay's hand and then pointed towards her. Chhavi's heartbeat raced.

'Baba knows whose plan it was to harm you in the campus the other day,' Vijay said. She stared at him silently.

'Gope was behind it. They were intimidated by your party and you. He won't leave them just like that,' he said, anger flushing his face.

Chhavi came forward. 'I have left campus politics as I had promised Baba. I have nothing to do with it now.'

'Then why did you go today?' Vijay asked sharply. She was uncomfortable with the question and kept quiet. She didn't know why they were discussing it here, and where was it leading to. She looked apologetically at her father who signalled at her brother once again; through his eyes.

'Chhavi,' Vijay cleared his throat. 'Baba knows that you had gone to Jalegar with that low caste; and not on an educational trip.' She was listless for a few moments before gathering herself.

'He had saved my life.'

Vijay was furious. 'So does that mean we let that chamar become our brother-in-law? Let him live in our house?'

'I love him,' she said at last. After a momentary paralysis that overtook everyone present, rage flew. Vijay was about to slap her when Baba stopped him by clutching his shirt sleeve. The nurse intervened seeing emotions getting out of hand.

'Please, you can do all this when the patient is out of the hospital. He has just been through a heart surgery,' she pleaded pointing towards the heart rate monitor. The green line beeped in succession, going up and down. Baba gestured at her to remove the mask. She declined. He requested her again; signalling for two minutes with his fingers.

'Chhavi,' he spoke slowly. 'It is said that a woman is born with three obligations into this world. The first is towards her father, the second towards her husband and the third towards her children. Whether you want to fulfil the first, depends on you.'

'Baba, love doesn't choose a caste; it chooses the heart,' she said.

'It's because of all your wrong-doings that has landed us and Baba here, in the ICU,' Vijay said heatedly. 'We should be throwing that boy out of this city.'

Baba gestured at him to calm down.

'You haven't answered my question,' Baba looked at her.

'Baba, I can't think of my life without him. Please meet him once,' she pleaded.

'There is no match between the two of you,' Baba was tiring up. The beep on the monitor was losing its momentum. 'You will have to choose one: your father or that Dalit boy.'

The nurse interrupted them, 'His heartbeat is dipping; he needs to be on the ventilator immediately.'

She looked at her helpless grandmother, her brothers: Vijay looked smothered with disgust, Anil uncertain and fearful.

'Are you going to kill him, Chhavi? Answer him,' Vijay blurted.

She gazed at Baba; how oddly different her last two visits to the hospital had been. One was to see a man who had saved her life, while the second to see another who wished to take it away. The two men she loved the most in her life.

'I choose you Baba,' the words escaped her mouth. Baba looked a bit comforted.

'I have fixed up your match with Pandeyji's son. He is a good, cultured boy,' Baba said.

'Marrying someone who I don't even know? What about my studies?' she asked, exhausted.

'You will get enough opportunities to know each other and you are not completing your graduation here; this place is too dangerous for you,' he said and coughed. The nurse put the oxygen mask back in its place.

'Whatever I do is for your good. Remember that,' he said, before the respiratory equipment blocked his speech. She nodded, devoid of any emotion, as if everything within her had dried up within those few minutes.

Abhay entered Gajaraj Singh Gope's room in haste, Bittu following him closely. Gope sat alone inside without any of his customary cronies there to humour him.

Gope was pensive and looked up. 'What brings you here?'

'That fucking son of a bitch has vomited openly in the campus,' he said hastily.

'What?' Gope got up, 'What has he spoken?'

Abhay sat down clasping his head. 'The bastard has gone ahead to join CSWI announcing in front of everyone... that he was merely a pawn acting at behest of other leaders.'

'Did he name us?' Gope asked slowly.

Abhay looked up. 'No bhaiya, but the damage is almost the same. Everyone knows that there are only two leaders in the campus: Tiwari and You.'

'Are students talking about it?'

Abhay nodded. 'Of course, won't they?' He looked at him as if he were a kid.

'A common student, acknowledging openly that he did everything for power, money, and fame will have a tremendous impact. He has set an example of himself.'

'Panditji has called me to meet him,' Gope mentioned out of the blue.

Abhay stammered. 'Why? When is this meeting?'

'I don't know why he has called for me. He had a heart

attack in the morning, but it seems he is fine now. As soon as he comes back home, I guess,' he looked at Abhay, whose face had turned pale all of a sudden.

Gope scratched his head. 'What that Dalit has gone and done is going to cost us in the elections.' Abhay nodded in affirmation.

He sat next to Abhay, fury rushing on his face like a torrent. 'Before we pay a price for his folly; Krishna will have to pay for his mistake.'

The hostel attendant knocked on Krishna's door, late at night. He came out.

'There's a call for you,' the attendant said wiping his nose.

'From home?' he asked.

'No, there is someone called Chhavi,' the attendant said. His heart missed a beat.

He raced towards the common room. It overflowed with students who were watching a one-day cricket match between England and India on the television. Sachin Tendulkar was on strike; students watched intently, awaiting action. Krishna picked up the receiver.

'Hello, Chhavi?'

'Krishna,' her voice sounding censored.

'How is Panditji?'

'Baba had a heart attack this morning. We were lucky to get him to the hospital in time.'

Krishna was jolted with the news. Sachin had hit a boundary; the room erupted in cheers.

'Is he fine now?'

'Yes, out of danger.'

'Krishna,' she said and then something else. Sachin had hit a six now, he was on a rampage. He couldn't hear her further in all the noise.

'Chhavi, I am sorry. There is too much noise here,' he said. Luckily, there was a break. Drinks came out into the ground. A soft drinks commercial started playing, overtaking the incoherent uproar of the students.

He didn't hear her reply, and repeated his last sentence.

She was weeping, sobbing, first in smaller bursts; and then when she couldn't control herself, crying aloud, gasping.

His daze continued. 'Chhavi, why are you crying?' he asked. The match had resumed, Sachin played on 88. India needed twenty-two runs more to win.

'Baba knows about us,' she said weeping.

'How does he?' He asked. There was an appeal for leg before wicket; the umpire ruled it not out. Sachin survived and the students heaved a joint sigh of relief.

'I had called him from your village, remember? He called me back on the same number to check on something and found out that it was an STD booth in Jalegar. Baba has the memory of an elephant; he remembered that you were from Jalegar.'

He cleared his throat, nervous enough; he didn't want to prod further. 'So?'

'I had to choose between you and him.'

Tears trickled down his eyes, in straight lines initially and then ran amok all over his face. He took a deep breath and turned around to face the wall, lest he would be seen. India needed seventeen more, Tendulkar was on 93. The students waited, huddled around the television, with baited breath.

'Let's talk about it when we meet,' he mumbled.

'They want me to get married. Before the end of this year,' she had stopped crying and spoke in a voice that sounded bankrupt.

The ugly ferocity of her words dawned into his being and made him howl. Three runs came through an overthrow; India was seven runs away from victory, and Tendulkar was on 99.

'What about me Chhavi? What about me?' he cried hoarsely as his tears battled with his voice. The euphoric chant of "Sachin... Sachin!" drowned his voice completely.

He couldn't hear what she said, as noise took over. Sachin had hit the penultimate ball for four; a century for him, and India had won. The students had started dancing on the bench, chairs, and the dining table of the common room. The pandemonium continued for a while and then they exited the room making merry; not noticing him standing in one corner with the phone receiver in his hand, crying, as if his heart had burst open.

He disconnected the phone after the noise had receded and walked back. It seemed as if he was walking through a quagmire. Every step that he took made him sink deeper into it.

The door was ajar when he entered his room. Gope sat on his cot with his legs crossed and his cronies around standing guard. He could recognize only Abhay and Bittu.

'Why are you here?' he asked Gope.

'Bastard, you think you can do whatever and no one can stop you,' Abhay lashed out.

'I have not harmed you personally bhaiya. If you still think I am at fault, you may do whatever,' he said facing Gope.

Gope slapped him as he got up. 'Mother fucker, I supported you completely, bloody low caste, and you dare to betray me.' Abhay and others getting the cue, pounced on him, punching him on the face, kicking him in the ribs. He was oblivious to everything; the least of it was pain.

'That bitch you saved that day has caused us enough discomfort. I wish she had died,' Gope sneered looking at Krishna getting beaten up mercilessly.

Gope's words pierced him deep within. He gathered all his might to push everybody around to pick up a glass bottle that rested in a corner. He lunged at Gope and caught him by the neck; the notorious campus leader looked terribly scared.

'Don't even mention her name bhaiya. Just leave,' he said placing the bottle on his neck.

'Krishna,' Gope said at the door. 'If I see you in the campus tomorrow, you are going to repent that moment till you live.'

Krishna was putting all his belongings into a cardboard box when Shiv entered the room.

'What are you up to chamar ke?' he joked.

'I can't stay here Shiv. I am going,' he said engrossed in the job.

Shiv looked shell-shocked. 'Where Krishna? Why?'

'You won't understand Shiv and I don't have time,' he said between dumping clothes and his belongings in the box, and wiping away tears that had lined up in his eyes.

'Where, Krishna?' Shiv asked sitting on the cot and clutching his head. 'Who has hurt you so badly?' he pointed at Krishna's face; blood trickled from his nose and lip. His forehead bled as well.

'Leave it! I am leaving this city,' he said hastily, wrapping the box with a cello tape.

'Where are you going Krishna?'

'Mumbai. Tomorrow. Pushpak Express in the evening.'

'And your studies?' Shiv asked.

'I want to work now,' he said. 'That box is for you. You may use it.'

'Do you have money to survive there?' Shiv asked. Krishna pulled the sheet over his face and chose not to answer.

Shiv left the room late in the night to inform Chhavi over the phone that Krishna was unstoppable, that he was leaving.

Chhavi waited at the Charbagh Railway Station on platform number 7. The weather had played truant and it had been raining since afternoon, auguring the nip in the air a bit earlier than expected; summers would soon dissolve into the winter season. She looked up at the staircase frequently to see passengers descending onto the platform.

She looked up again and saw him walking down. He just had his cotton bag hanging across his shoulders. It looked full; maybe he had tucked a few clothes inside. But beyond that, he carried nothing. He looked sadder than she had ever seen him and more tired than ever before. Suddenly she felt a terrible guilt welling up inside that nudged tears that her eyes had held back. They rolled over her cheeks. He held the railing and took measured steps, not looking up even once, but staring into the ground.

He looked up when his feet landed on the platform. She could see bruises on his forehead. There was a deep gash on his lower lip; blood had dried up over it and some on his chin. His eyes were swollen, lack of sleep and a bounty of sorrow seemed like the only reason. He was limping a bit and walked further away from her on the platform when she called his name. In between a million other sounds on the station, he heard her in the first go, as if he longed to hear her voice. He turned back a bit reluctantly, and as he looked into her eyes, both Chhavi and Krishna could feel each other's pain. He walked towards her slowly, not letting her go out of sight even for a moment.

She touched the bruise on his forehead and the gash on his lip gently. He felt the tenderness of her touch on his skin.

'You aren't taking anything else?' she asked touching his bag.

'What will I do with more? This is enough.'

She handed him a piece of paper. writerKK@hotmail.com was scribbled on it along with krishnaandchhavi.

'What is this?' he asked.

'I have opened an e-mail account for you; writerkk@hotmail.com is your address.'

'KK?' he asked.

'It's short for Krishna Kumar. Once you become a famous writer, your name will be a bit long for others to say. KK is crisper and hip,' she attempted to smile, failing in the end.

'The other is your password - krishnaandchhavi. Once you log in to your account, the computer will ask for a password which is this. Will you be able to handle?' she asked.

'I will learn, Chhavi,' he said. She nodded.

He looked up to speak but choked in his tears. She held his hand. 'Krishna?'

'If it wasn't for my caste and poverty, no one could have separated us. No Chhavi?' he sobbed.

'No Krishna,' she said weeping alongside him. 'Did I ruin your life?'

'You infused love and hope into my life; there couldn't be anything better in it.'

She led him to sit on the platform bench. He cradled his head on her lap as she ran her fingers through his hair.

Tears kept flowing out of their eyes till both of them were completely drained. The PA system crackled, announcing the arrival of Pushpak Express.

'Krishna,' she said. He looked up at her; his head still on her lap.

'Don't let our love lose. I am letting you go because I know this will make you stronger. I couldn't do this with my father, letting him go; it would have killed him.'

He lifted himself up.

'How will I live without you, so many miles away? Alone?' he asked.

'I am not leaving you even for a moment,' she said. He couldn't understand what she had meant. The train had nestled up on the railway tracks, passengers crowding at the doors, in a momentous hurry to enter the coupe.

'Unlock the unique potential that you possess, Krishna. It's right here,' she poked his chest that covered his heart.

'Will you talk to me sometimes?' he asked.

She shook her head. 'No, never. It will weaken us. Both of us have to walk this path alone, against all odds.'

'Will we ever meet?' he said, the final moments of separation lurking above them. She did not answer.

'Here,' she took out a lunch box from her bag. 'You will need it on the way. Don't eat station food.'

The train blew the horn and started moving, passengers waving goodbyes to the loved ones.

'I have to leave,' his eyes saying, that he never wanted to.

'Krishna,' she said. He stopped dead in his tracks.

'We are tied together with this invisible rope,' she gestured with her hands looking at him. 'However far you may wander, it will still remain tied, to me, at one end. You will never lose me Krishna, and there will be a day when I will pull you back.'

'I will wait for that day,' he said running towards the train that sped with each passing moment.

He opened the lunch box after the train had crossed Jhansi Junction. It carried food in two casseroles, but the last one looked empty. He uncovered the lid; there was a bundle of currency notes and a hand-written note. He straightened the piece of paper – 'I know you wouldn't like it Krishna, but this is a small loan. Please accept it and promise to repay me, very soon.'

He nodded to himself and cried uncontrollably, sitting next to the bathroom of the general compartment, with her lunch box in his hands.

Ram Singh took his eyes away from the road and glanced at KK.

'There is no pain that hurts more than separating from someone you love, sahib,' he said. 'More so when you know that this could well be the last time.'

It was past midnight and the highway was relatively less crowded with mostly trucks plying on it. They had crossed Jhansi a while ago, driving almost nonstop.

'Love is a double-edged sword, Ram Singh. It has the ability to push you into the deepest of hells and also the power to redeem you from it.'

'What did you do to reach so far? How could you not let sorrow overpower your future?' Ram Singh asked.

'I didn't do much, our love did,' KK said watching the road.

Krishna alighted at the Mumbai Central Station the next night. He checked his watch: 10.00 p.m. He walked out of the station, looking around. He could see a huge sea of people wherever he looked; it was an unbelievable sight. He felt hungry; her lunch box could only last till afternoon. Perhaps he had eaten more than his usual self. Food carts were lined up on one side, amply lit, selling bhel puri, idli, vada sambhar, misal, and vada pav. He glanced at their aluminium menus hanging on the cart's frame. He settled for two vada pavs and a cup of tea, the cheapest option. The bundle of currency notes he had accepted as a loan rested in the inner pocket of his trousers. It comforted him. He had not counted them, knowing well that they would be enough to support him for at least a few days. He kept sitting on the pavement looking at the busy street where the crowd grew thinner with each passing hour. He thought of his life that he had left behind in Lucknow, how it had changed completely over the last forty-eight hours. Chhavi didn't leave him even for a moment since the time he saw her last at the station. It was as if his mind and heart had reconstructed themselves, into two distinct halves. One half was only reserved for her while every other memory or emotion was left to occupy the other.

It was well over midnight. He looked around at the benches on the street; all were occupied. He got up and walked back into the station; it was still as crowded. It seemed as if all the people who walked there a few hours back had decided to take a small nap on the station itself. He searched and found some space near a pillar that had turned maroon tolerating stains over the years. He lied down on the floor and shut his eyes.

The clamour of the hawkers woke him up early in the morning. He took directions of a public toilet from the tea vendor while paying him for a cup. He washed himself up and changed into a fresh set of clothes in just two rupees. He showed the piece of paper that had the address of the advertising agency scribbled on it to the toilet attendant.

'Parel is not very far. Just follow your nose; you will hit Jacob Circle, go straight from there,' he said.

'What would the distance be?' Krishna asked hesitatingly.

'It's about five or six kilometres. But why do you ask this? There is a direct bus.'

Krishna looked at his watch. It was just seven in the morning. He chose to walk.

He reached the C&M office a few minutes after eight. The office occupied three floors of the Oberoi Towers, a colossal building with a transparent glass façade. He was greeted by a barren reception; the wall behind highlighted the oversized C&M logo. He looked around the desolate space and then sat down on the cushioned sofa. The guard was buttoning his uniform shirt when he noticed him.

'You will have to come at ten for the courier; there are still some packets that need to be done with,' the guard said mistaking him for a courier boy.

Krishna got up and walked towards him. 'No. I want meet Virag Joshi actually,' he said.

The guard stared first at him and then at his watch, 'Have you seen your watch? Who comes so early for work and that too in an advertising agency?'

Krishna didn't know what to say. 'By when is he expected?'

'Depends at what time Joshiji would have left last night. This is agency culture,' the guard said displaying his innate intelligence. 'It seems that you are from Bihar. Aren't you?' he added. Krishna nodded.

He clapped with both his hands, 'I could figure that out from your accent. Which part?'

'District Darbhangha.'

'Good. It's nice meeting one of your people right in the morning.' He stretched his hand out. Krishna shook his hand.

'Where are you coming from?' he asked

'Lucknow.'

'Why do you want to meet Joshiji?'

'I am looking for a job.'

The guard nodded his head seriously; as if he were listening to a sermon.

'Would you like to have tea and something to eat?' he asked as if he owned the place. Krishna said yes, hesitatingly.

Virag Joshi entered the office at eleven. By then, the fair twenty-something girl, responsible for manning the reception had taken her place and the guard was pushed ahead on the stool near the gate. Virag was humming a song and whistling along as he entered; he looked only a few years elder to him. The guard interrupted his stroll to whisper something.

He looked in Krishna's direction. 'Hi. Have you been waiting for me?'

Krishna nodded. 'Chhavi Mishra, your cousin from Lucknow had asked me to meet you. I am looking for a job.'

Virag held a dramatic expression on his face. 'She spoke to me just a few days back and you are here already?' He took out a strange looking instrument from his pocket, rectangular and pressed some keys on it. He had read about it in Lucknow, but never seen one. It was called a mobile phone. One could talk with anyone, anytime and anywhere in the world. He wished if Chhavi and he could have it.

'Follow me,' he signalled and started whistling again. The office looked wondrous, something that he had never seen before, done up wholly in two colours, red and green. The logo of C&M – Charles and Mayor had the same colours as well. Perhaps the agency owners fancied red and green. The cubicles were neatly arranged in straight lines and at some places into small clusters. On their walls under the board pins, different advertisements dangled; the ones that are seen in newspapers. The graffitied walls had queer stuff written over them: *If the client doesn't buy what you are trying to sell, throw it in the dustbin*; *Creative minds are the Devil's nest*; *Do not fall in love here. She is going to leave you for your boss*; *We don't hire creative people here. We hire people who can do business.* Krishna glanced at many such lines as he walked, some of them made sense, while others didn't. Everybody working in the office looked happy and young. There wasn't any who was graying. The way they dressed was unfamiliar even by Lucknow standards. An odd girl wearing a particular dress looked recognizable as Chhavi would have worn it sometime when he was with her.

'So what can you do for an advertising agency?' Virag tapped his shaved head. He sat in his cubicle with Krishna.

'I can write,' he replied.

He thought for a moment and pulled out some papers from his drawer.

'Are you comfortable with English?' he could sense Krishna's discomfort with the language.

'I write in Hindi.'

Virag nodded and handed him one of the papers. 'This ad's is written in English. Can you translate it in Hindi?'

It was an advertisement of coconut hair oil. It nourished a woman's hair like no other oil could, eased her of the tiredness, and made her super active again. There were three lines written at the bottom in English. He read each word carefully, some he couldn't understand, but broadly figured out what they meant. He took out his pen and started writing.

'Is this your first job after college?' Virag asked, sipping tea from his cup. Krishna nodded without raising his head. He handed the paper back to Virag who went through what he had written and handed him another one.

This time it was a motorcycle advertisement. One could ride about a hundred kilometres with just one litre of fuel and the vehicle looked great too. It sounded unbelievable! A hundred kilometres in a litre. But he focused on the translation instead.

Virag handed him the last sheet. It was for a face cream that made a woman look fairer, transformed her skin colour from dusky to milky white. Chhavi didn't need such products; she had been god gifted as far as matters of complexion were concerned, he thought.

Virag read all the three ad translations once again. 'You write well Krishna. The issue is your shortcoming with the English language.'

'I will learn.'

Virag thought for a couple of minutes. 'Ok! You are on as a Trainee Copy Writer.'

'Copy-writer?' Krishna asked.

Virag smiled. 'Yes, the guy who writes the story in an advertisement.'

'What will the company pay me?' he asked. Virag didn't expect this abrupt question.

'It should be around three thousand bucks. Is that fine?'

'Yes, very much,' Krishna replied.

'Ok then. I will ask our HR department to get your appointment letter processed,' Virag said.

'Sir,' Krishna said, 'Can I make another request?'

'Don't call me sir. Or for that matter anyone else in this office. We call each other by the first name. That's the culture here.'

Krishna nodded.

'Can you help me with a place to stay? I can pay a little rent,' he said.

Virag laughed. 'Nothing is tougher than getting a roof over your head here. I wouldn't know much about this, but let me ask Anand, our administration head.' He picked up the phone.

The phone conversation lasted for a couple of minutes; he talked in English and mostly in monosyllables. Virag shook his head as he put the receiver down.

'No boss. There isn't a place that they know of,' he said. Krishna nodded, thinking about the space at the railway station again.

'There is one option though, but I have told him that you may not want to take it,' he said hesitatingly. Krishna looked at him eagerly.

'The guard who used to be here on the night duty has left recently. Though there is nothing much to keep an eye on, as the building has its own security; his only job was to see that any accident doesn't happen...like fire or theft. There is a small room behind the pantry that is allotted to the two guards, the night guard used to stay there.'

'I have no problems in doing that. How much do I need to pay for the room?' Krishna asked.

'Nothing. On the contrary, you will be paid two thousand bucks in addition. But are you really sure about this?' Virag asked.

'Thank you. I am one hundred percent sure.' Krishna smiled a bit.

The room was almost one-fourth the size of his hostel room in Lucknow. There was just a mattress on the floor and a bottle of water. The room couldn't take more than that. Cooking wasn't allowed, but one who stayed there could use the office pantry for his evening meal. Krishna had spent his day in going through the files with cuttings of various advertisements that C&M had created over the years. The ads were neatly arranged client-wise. He could make out that the agency had enough clients to run its house. In the evening, he had gone out to the nearby local market to buy some necessities, a couple of vegetables, rice and some pulses. It had been a fair day; he was employed, hoping to earn five thousand rupees a month and had a place to stay that came free. He could also send some money home now.

The room was noisy and had a small window that opened to face a flyover. The vehicles zipped all through the day, blowing piercing horns, and throwing smoke away. It would subside as the night would progress, he said to himself, digging out his last night's memory of watching traffic. He took out the diary from his bag, flipped through the pages, and found a blank space on one of them. He wished if he could speak to her once, just once. Sadness gripped his heart again as he shut his eyes.

'Krishna,' she said as he woke up from his nap. She was sitting right in front, on the mattress. Looking at him lovingly. 'Why don't you write?'

'I just can't.'

'Then would you let go of that one unique thing that you possess, that millions of others don't?' she asked.

'How can my hand move if my heart is sad,' he said.

'If you can use your sadness as a source of growth, you will become a writer of greater depth. Even more wonderful than you currently are,' she said.

He picked up his pen again and started writing.

यह जो सुनहरी सी धूप छिटकी है मेरे ऊपर
यह कर रही होगी कहीं तुम्हारे तन को भी उज्ज्वल
मेरे चेहरे से खेलती और फिर राह बदलती यह शरारती हवा
उड़ाती होगी तुम्हारे दुपट्टे को भी दाएँ बाएँ, कितनी ही बार
बादलों के साथ दौड़ लगाते यह तमाम पंछी
शायद तुम्हारी खिड़की के सिरहाने भी पनाह पाते होंगे
यह जो मीलों का फासला अब बन चुका है हमारे बीच
उसका पहला पत्थर तो तुम्हारा पाँव अब भी छूता होगा

It had taken him seven days to realize that the city of Mumbai was different. He had been sitting in an office that had more than two hundred people, yet besides general chit-chatting with a few, no one had burdened him with unnecessary questions. Where did he come from? What his name was and his surname, and most critically, his caste. Everyone seemed to be doing their own thing, busy running their own lives. He had undergone some basic training sessions in the office, conducted by different departments: code of conduct in C&M, rules and regulations to be followed, client handling and communication. He would spend most of his days going through the thick ad files or watching television commercials made by C&M that ran in a loop on the television screen at the reception. The visual story that these commercials told was fascinating to him. Late evenings would go in preparing meals in the borrowed pantry; and nights either writing in his notebook or counting days and hours that had passed, before he last saw her.

Virag had been travelling for the last three days but had come to the office today. He was the Creative Director of Mumbai branch, the HR manager had told him, and managed close to forty clients.

Virag tapped his shoulder. 'So how have you been doing Krishna? Have you gone through all of this?' he pointed at the ad files.

'Yes. All of them,' Krishna said getting up.

'Good. So now that your training is over; let's get in to the real world.'

'Shibani!' He shouted across the hall. A cute looking girl with short hair turned around. Krishna had noticed her earlier; one of those cheerful, backslapping people. Boys like her existed in the university, perpetually smiling, happy with life, but she was the first girl he had seen with that attitude.

'Yes baldy. When did you get back from Bangalore?' she replied back with an equal decibel.

'Just today, darling; and please stay there. Don't disappear,' he signalled at Krishna to follow him.

'I want you to meet Krishna,' Virag introduced him. 'He is a rookie who will help us with copy.'

'Hi Krishna! I am Shibani. Welcome to C&M.' She smiled as they shook hands.

'I was hoping if he could work on some of your clients,' Virag said.

'Can he do both Hindi and English copy?' she asked sizing him up.

Virag looked at him. 'Hindi as of now. He is good at that.'

Krishna interrupted, 'I can give English a try too.'

She looked amused. 'Great. Those Malani Tea guys are really panicking, because we haven't delivered on their new brief. In fact, I was just going to have a team meeting on it. Can he join us?'

'He is all yours, dear,' Virag replied.

She put her arm around Krishna's shoulders, 'Let's get going then.'

He entered the conference room with her arm still dangling around his shoulder and her touch making him uncomfortable. He was not used to others touching him much since birth, and especially a woman.

'Guys, meet Krishna. He is the new copy writer that we have hired and his first project is Rahul's Malani Tea,' she chuckled looking at one of the guys in the room.

'What is this Shibani, here you are amused at my helplessness, and there that Mr. Malani has been roasting my ass for the last two meetings. I am telling you frankly, if we don't get it right this time, this client is walking out for good,' Rahul said frustratingly. There were five of them in the room, including Shibani and him. The other two besides Rahul looked like his juniors.

'But why does he want to change his tag line, it's good – *India Ka Kadak Taste*,' Shibani exclaimed. 'These clients, I tell you. Just because they get bored with something, put the blame on their consumers and ask their agency to give them something different,' she stressed.

'If we don't get his 'Different' tagline soon, it will make him indifferent towards us.' Rahul scratched his sweaty forehead.

Shibani turned towards Krishna. 'Can we look at something new and refreshing? We have this account with us for over three years now and when the team handles it for so long, new ideas stop coming. We keep recycling the same old shit.'

Krishna nodded. 'Can I see some of the old stuff that we have done?' he asked.

Shibani interrupted, 'But don't use that as a reference; create something new.'

Rahul took a deep breath and looked at Krishna. 'Ok, in that case, let's give it one last try. I will e-mail the creative to you. I have a meeting on Wednesday, so we have six days left, including today. If we can crack the copy latest by day after, then the designers can make the creative over the next two days.'

'I will finish by then,' Krishna said.

'These files are heavy, Rahul. Our servers aren't equipped for this. Give him hard copies instead,' Shibani said.

He sat on the mattress in his room. The noise and the dust had now become his friendly everyday invader; filling all the empty spaces in his room. The incandescent bulb flickered over his head, suffering the low voltage. He thought of Chhavi a distance away, and wondered if things around her reminded her of him the way they brought her memories back to him. When she walked inside the campus gates, did she still see him sitting on the stairs, in the library or with him in front of various department buildings? Did she think about him when she sat in an auto rickshaw or when she passed the Hanuman Temple on the Gomti Bridge? When she opened her eyes in the morning, did her consciousness pull her towards him first and before she allowed sleep to numb her senses at night, did he become her last memory?

तुम्हें भूलना अब एक नयी सिरदर्दी है
मेरे उस हर एक पल को, जिसमें तुम्हारा कुछ न कुछ छूटा है
हर उस जगह को, जिसमें तुम्हारी खुशबू अब भी बसी है
हर गली को, जिसमें तुम्हारी पैरों से छिटकी धूल अब भी बिखरी है
तुम्हारे चेहरे को, जिसको मेरी आँखे खुलते ही ढूँढ़ती है
तुम्हारे साथ होने के अहसास को, जिसके बिना मैं खुद गुमशुदा हूँ

He kept his pen down and shut his diary. He began rummaging through the files containing advertisements of Malani Tea. He scribbled a few words on the paper: Malani Tea – Kick starts your day, *Taazgi* (freshness), wakes you up, connects people, relationships, health and habit. He circled two out of them – relationships and connects people.

He struggled for a couple of hours before writing two lines of copy and fell down with exhaustion.

Malani Tea – Ghole Rishton Main Mithaas (Mixes sweetness into your relationships).

Malani Tea – Har Ghoont Kare Rishte Mazboot (Every sip of it strengthens your relationships).

Krishna was now about a couple of months old in Mumbai and his views about C&M and the city had widened. Both of them were fussy about their weekends. If there wasn't work that could kill, no employee wanted to work after four in the evenings on Fridays in C&M. Mumbai also changed its demeanour overnight. The mad rush that jutted out on the streets through weekdays would sublimate over Saturdays and Sundays. People would discover that they could laugh, walk leisurely in markets, parks and on the pavements, eat in peace at roadside cafes alone, or with their families. Krishna had the Arabian Sea at his disposal on weekends. On Saturdays, he would take a bus to Haji Ali, drink a glass of juice, and then walk to Nariman point. There he would sit for hours, looking at the sea, on the ledge that had grown from the stone laden pavement running across the length of the ocean. He would see the faded sun sinking behind gigantic ships, small boats and flocks of birds going back home after the day's adventure. He would think of Lucknow, his hostel room, Shiv and their banter, his younger brother and sometimes of his mother. His past would call out for him repeatedly as he sat there, tempting him to return; for he was more comfortable there, than the unseen future that he hadn't seen as yet. Chhavi would be sitting next to him on the ledge, her hand resting on his, looking at the sea. Krishna would seldom turn around to ask her:

'I feel like going back to where I came from.'

'Where would that be?' she asked.

'Lucknow, or back to my village in Jalegar. I feel so lonely here and uncertain about my future in this unknown land.'

'So you want to go back to your past that you never really liked?' she asked gazing at him. 'Didn't you yearn to turn your future better and bright?'

He nodded, to get irritated suddenly. 'I have limitations. I didn't know about them that time.'

She caressed his palm gently. 'Self limitations are the decisions that we take, to limit ourselves and the potential we possess.

'Persevere some more. For every action that you take now is going to shape the future,' she said.

He would get up and walk back to Parel late in the night on Saturday and then write the whole day on Sunday.

C&M was getting fond of his work and consistent recognition had started coming his way. The Malani Tea meeting went off very well; Rahul's tight hug to him said it all. The owner loved the new tag lines; especially *Ghole Rishton Main Mithaas*. The owner said it reminded him of having tea in the morning with their relatives in their small house in Jodhpur a couple of decades back. They were struggling to make their ends meet then. The C&M team went out to a classy Chinese restaurant in the evening. Everything was on the house; you could order anything to eat or drink. Krishna settled for vodka and ate to his heart's content, after endless meals of dal, rice and a vegetable. This was his second visit to a fancy restaurant, pretty soon after his last with Chhavi about ninety-six days back, on her birthday. He tried to recollect what she had ordered at Chung Fa, the waiter towering over him. He ordered Chilly Chicken and Honey Potato. Towards the end of the dinner, Shibani gifted him with a pen that looked expensive, wrapped in a beautiful box. Krishna was happy because his old pen was wearing away and he had a lot more to write.

Shibani had started putting a lot of trust in Krishna. He had started working on all her clients so much so that if Virag attempted to pull him onto some other account that didn't belong to her, she would get offended.

'Baldy, I love him. Why do you want to drive us apart?' she said theatrically, holding Krishna's hand.

Virag shook his head desperately, 'He needs to work on other brands as well, sweetie.'

She raised her eyebrows. 'Who handles the maximum business at C&M?' Virag fell silent.

She pulled Krishna inside the conference room. 'If that happens to be me, my dear, then shouldn't I be getting the first preference?'

The C&M team had occupied the conference room. She connected her laptop with the projector and opened up a presentation.

'Sweet Beat is a Belgian sweetener launching in India, starting with Delhi and Bombay.'

'How is it different from other sweeteners already existing in the market?' Rohit asked. He looked after Strategy and Planning.

'Good question. The biggest one is, that unlike other sweeteners that are used only for replacing sugar in tea and coffee, this one can actually be used like sugar.'

'What do you mean by that?' Rohit asked.

'You can add it to all kinds of sweets; ice-creams, pudding, and custard...just like you add sugar. Almost zero calorie, hundred percent natural, and no aspartame.'

This pleased Rohit. 'That sounds like a real differentiator. We can do a good pitch with this. No Krishna?' Krishna nodded.

Rohit stroked his chin. 'India is a leading producer of sugar in the world. We use it in most of the things we eat and drink – from many cups of tea or coffee that we take, to sweets and ice creams, custard, cakes and even curd.'

'It's an indulgence that we just can't do without,' Krishna added, 'but these sweets or meetha as it is called in our country, also comes with a large set of problems.'

'Yeah, I mean this country has the highest number of diabetic patients in the world, add to that one out of three Indians suffering from high BP,' Shibani said nodding her head.

Rohit got up to stand near the board. 'Don't forget the rising obesity Shibani. So people do want to consume sweets, but because of sugar in it, feel guilty after they have had one. That's a paradox.' The conference room submerged into silence.

Krishna cleared his throat, 'Eating sweets today then is akin to a sin. Our proposition for Sweet Beat – that is much healthier and adds more taste than other sweeteners – should be about how the consumers can "undo this sin" when they use it.'

Rohit clapped his hands together, elatedly. 'That seems like a good platform that you can work on, Krishna. And the one who buys it will mostly be the lady of the house.'

Shibani nodded. 'I like it too. But Sweet Beat isn't the best as far as taste goes.'

'In advertising, you are allowed to take some liberties with the consumer, madam.' Rohit smiled.

They drove for the Sweet Beat Presentation in Virag's car. The meeting was at the owner's bungalow that also served as his weekend getaway in Lonavla. It was the first time that Krishna was going with the C&M team for a pitch meeting. He sat next to Virag who was driving; Shibani and Rahul sat at the back. The expressway that connected Mumbai with Pune had been recently constructed; work on some patches was still going on. They zipped at a speed of hundred. Shibani looked pretty, wearing a pink top and jeans that hugged her body well, and a pair of black sunglasses. Chhavi used to wear the same combination sometimes, he remembered, and then gazed at the small hills getting left behind as the car raced ahead.

'Hope you are carrying all the hard copies of the artworks along with mock-ups,' Shibani said looking at Rahul.

He had dozed off and woke up abruptly. 'Yes, they are all in Puneet's car.' His team mates trailed them in another car.

'How much time do you think it will take Shibani?' Virag asked stopping his whistle midway.

She looked at her watch, 'If we reach there by one, we should be done by four-four-thirty tops.'

Virag nodded and looked ahead as the car approached a tunnel. 'I have heard there are quite a few of these and pretty long ones,' he looked at the rear view mirror.

Shibani shrugged. 'No idea boss. This is my first time on this expressway.'

'Chhavi got married yesterday. Did you wish her?' Virag looked at Krishna as he switched on the car headlights. Krishna was lost in his thought; he hadn't heard what Virag had said.

'What did you say?' He looked at Virag. The tunnel was right ahead, Virag looked at it attentively.

'Chhavi got married yesterday. It's a pity that our family couldn't attend. Did you wish her?' Virag said as the car entered the waiting darkness inside the tunnel.

He couldn't hold the sudden rush of tears that erupted from his eyes and swept down his face. He wanted to answer Virag, but his voice choked. He wiped his tears away from the other hand.

'Who are we talking about?' Shibani asked.

The tunnel was left behind. Virag switched off the headlights. 'A Cousin of mine from Lucknow. She also happens to be Krishna's friend. She had referred him for a job at C&M,' Virag replied.

'Oh! Then we should thank her for a wonderful find,' she slapped Krishna's shoulder.

The Chandok Getaway had a small but classy conference room in their five-star resort-like getaway. The owners, Pradeep Chandok and his ultra chic wife seemed to be equally involved in the Sweet Beat launch. Danny, the CEO of the parent Belgian company was also present. Shibani started the presentation, with Rahul and Virag pitching in wherever it was required. It had been pre-decided that Shibani would take them through the C&M credentials, sweetener industry market, and the Indian opportunity. After which Virag would talk about competition, the consumer insight, and finally the creative route for Sweet Beat. Krishna looked blankly at the screen, the voices of Shibani and Virag whirring in his ears, his mind indifferent to the conversation.

'With Sweet Beat in your life, no need to feel guilty anymore, as you gorge on your favourite sweets and endless cups of tea and coffee. For Sweet Beat doesn't just taste good, but is healthy too. Zero calorie, hundred percent natural and no aspartame,' Virag was just about to unveil the tag line. Rahul got up with his team holding the creative's and laying them on the table.

'*Sweet Beat – Ab Wahi Meetha, Health Ke Saath*,' he announced dramatically.

The three of them looked attentively at the artworks. Pradeep Chandok looked convinced; his wife had a weird expression on her face, while Danny nodded questioningly.

"What's *meetha*?' Danny asked. Shibani had talked about the relevance of Meetha in Indian culture before, but she went through it again.

'Who calls sweet a *meetha* these days?' the wife asked unconvincingly.

'All homes, madam, where eating sweets is a habit,' Virag butted in.

The wife shook her head tentatively, her diamond studded earrings chimed. 'Not homes where Sweet Beat will go. It's going to be the most expensive product in the category. The tag line needs to be classier, hip, and sexy.' She looked at Danny.

Danny raised his hands in the air, 'Well the advertising needs to be sexy of course, or else how would people notice!' he said, non-committal.

The owner, Pradeep Chandok picked up one of the creatives. 'It's called Meetha at all my friends' houses though.'

His wife snapped. 'Your friends are all from Aligarh, that tiny island you belong to. Have you ever seen any of my friends calling it meetha?' The husband recoiled.

Shibani saw that conversation wasn't going anywhere; it required an intervention, in line with the client's wish. She glanced at Krishna. 'Can we tweak it a bit so that it sounds classy?' Everyone's eyes turned towards him as Krishna struggled to keep his mind in check.

'What's classy about eating a sweet? You eat them because you love them, be it Aligarh or Mumbai. It's a part of Indian tradition for thousands of years; and we all have grown up eating Meetha,' he rattled.

The wife raised her eyebrow, her face not appreciative of his comment. 'And where have you grown up?'

Krishna paused. 'In Bihar, Madam.'

The wife smiled sarcastically. 'Bihar? So, there it goes guys. Has he written this?' she waved the creative around. The moments where overwhelming; everybody stayed quiet.

'If you guys are looking at someone from back of beyond to work on Sweet Beat, it doesn't seem to work,' she said throwing away the creative on the table. Krishna sat there motionless, grasping failure.

Virag attempted a last ditch effort. 'You remember a tag line, Mrs. Chandok, that is simple just because the simplicity sticks to you.

The wife was steely, discarding Virag's remark. 'You are losing time, C&M. Your copy is too safe. We need something edgy,' she said looking at Krishna. Her husband and Danny got up looking uncomfortable. The meeting ended.

This perhaps could have been the worst day of his life; both his mind and heart slaughtered together. No one spoke about the meeting in the car. For Krishna, it seemed he faced a dead end and all that was left was to collapse and surrender. Virag left him at the office building in Parel, along with Shibani, for she stayed in Worli.

'Do you stay somewhere close to Parel?' Shibani asked. He pointed at the C&M building. She looked unsure about what he meant.

'I stay in the office, in the room behind the pantry.'

She was shocked, but didn't let it show.

She held his hand. 'Don't think about it too much; you will get to face worse than them. Just believe that you are good,' she said waving at an auto rickshaw.

He nodded; his face clayed with insult and rejection.

He entered his room and opened the window. Some light from the flyover siphoned its way into the room.

She stood near the window pane looking at him caringly.

'Are you hurt?'

He hit the window frame with his wrist, in anger. 'Wouldn't I be? You are married and happy. What if you forget me and your promise?'

She stepped forward. 'Look at me Krishna. Look into my eyes. Can I deceive you?' He looked into them, they were serene, and all that he could see was love for him.

He sat down on the mattress, cupping his face, looking at the ground. 'I am too small a fry in this gigantic sea, Chhavi. I will never succeed, however hard I may try.'

'Are you dejected with the outcome of your meeting today?'
He nodded.

'Krishna, do you remember the story of the little parrot I
had told you in the train?' she asked.

'I had fallen asleep soon after you had started. I don't
remember,' he replied. She smiled shaking her head.

*A long time ago there lived a parrot in a beautiful forest. The
forest gave shelter and protection to everyone. One day, there
was a thunderstorm and a dead tree was struck by its lightning.
The tree started burning and soon the fire caught up with
everything else in the forest. The animals of the forest were
scared and they ran amok. The parrot flew up high to escape
but when it saw the fellow animals crying in the fire, the parrot
decided to help them. It flew down to the nearby river and after
dipping into it, flew back to the forest and started sprinkling
water on the raging fire.*

*The little parrot attempted this many times and since it was
so exhausting, the parrot was about to collapse and die. This
shook the heavens and the gods looked down, watching who
was doing the hard work. One of the gods took the form of an
eagle and descended, flying along with the parrot. The eagle
advised the little parrot that it was a futile exercise and being
so small, it would not be able to save anyone. The eagle told
the parrot to fly away. The parrot disagreed and said – I will
still try. The eagle was so touched by the parrot's sincerity and
determination that tears started flowing out from its eyes.*

*The tears were magical, because they turned into raindrops
and fell on the forest fire. Soon the ravaging flames died down
and the forest became smokeless and everyone survived. The
little parrot that lay almost dead in one corner rejoiced as its*

burnt feathers grew in multi-coloured hues. The god said, 'You are never alone and small till you stop trying. Keep persevering as I stand next to you, for you will create a wonderful future.'

She ended the story. 'If you work tirelessly towards what you have set out to achieve with a pure heart, however insignificant you may be, even the gods will help you.' He still looked beaten.

'Krishna,' she said gaping at him. 'You can't give up even if you fall badly. You have to push yourself to stand up again and walk to your destination. This journey....you have to complete it. For us.'

He stared outside of the window. 'Do you see how tough the circumstances are? I will fall so many times that one day I may not have the energy to rise.'

'You can't change your circumstances Krishna, but what you can, is how you deal with them. If you continue to challenge and walk even one step a time, with a hope to succeed, the circumstances will have to change.'

He could feel every word that she spoke dissolve into his heart. He turned to look at her, but by then, she was already gone.

Krishna was more at ease since then, as he immersed himself completely in work. It had been close to a week since the Sweet Beat meeting. Shibani had told him that they were pushing the client to give them another chance, to present again. Krishna had gladly accepted to help, provided that Mrs. Chandok wasn't told that he had worked on it one more time. He had laughed along with the others.

He was culling out some information from the internet on the detergent industry at his workstation. Shibani had taught him how to use the internet and check office e-mails. He read all the e-mails, but replied only to a few, his English still not up to the mark. He accessed his Hotmail account that she had opened for him. It was empty.

Someone hugged him from behind. He turned around to see it was Shibani. She hugged him even tighter.

'We have got the Sweet Beat account. Yay!' she raised her hands up in the air; her team-mates surrounding her, hi-fived. Virag overheard the noise and joined them.

'Did the other agency presentations go worse?' he said jokingly.

'This was surreal,' she said disbelievingly. 'Pradeep Chandok called me up in the morning, apologetic as hell. You guys should have heard how he sounded.'

Everyone was eager to know more. 'He says that they thought about our creative route over and over again; and decided that the tagline that we had suggested is most apt for the Sweet Beat launch.'

'That's bull!' Virag said with disbelief, 'This can't be a result of intellectual stimulation. There *has* to be something else.'

'I know that baldy,' she held Virag's hand. 'He opened up when I coaxed him. Apparently they had a family get-together hosted by his trophy wife. There were close to a hundred people who attended, most of them addressing a sweet as meetha.'

Virag laughed. 'So was that enough to convince the wife?'

'Come on Virag!' she said dramatically. 'They sleep together, don't they? The rest Pradeep Chandok would have managed there. Isn't he a smart businessman?' she guffawed.

Virag patted Krishna. 'So, your charm eventually worked on her. No?'

Krishna smiled. 'Not my charm. God helped,' he said recalling Chhavi's story.

They celebrated the Sweet Beat win in a swanky restaurant, Not Just Jazz By The Bay at Marine Drive. A jazz band played inside, led by a tall woman in her mid-forties, wearing a body-hugging black dress and donning a layer of thick maroon lipstick. The singer sashayed on the beat gently as she sang to a captivated audience. The C&M team sat in an enclosure that had been customized for them in one corner, pleasuring their senses with music. An assortment of dishes lay on the table. Krishna sat there for a while and then got up to come outside on the pavement. He gazed at the sea for it fascinated him each time that he set his eyes on it.

Shibani came out and wrapped her arm around his waist. He felt uncomfortable with her touch and stayed rooted to the ground.

'What are you doing here?'

'I like the sea more than the music.'

She laughed. 'How can you be so transparent with what you feel most of the times?'

He paused. 'You are more transparent than me any day. It has taken me years to be able to say what I want to.'

'Haven't you spent your childhood in a village?'

He nodded gently.

'Village life would be so exciting, no?' she asked childlike.

'Yes, it was,' he said reminiscing about a few bits from his morbid village life.

'Have you fallen in love ever?' she asked, her arm still wrapped around. He nodded.

Her smile weakened. 'Is she in Mumbai?' He shook his head.

'I have loved once before. It broke my heart,' she said with a tear in her eye.

'Where is she? The one you love,' she asked.

'I don't know. She got married a while back,' he said.

She laughed uncontrollably as if she was relieved to hear this. 'And you still love her? I am sorry, but get real Krishna. Let's go inside, the team would be missing us.' She pulled him inside, holding his hand.

Krishna chose to go inside than testify for his love.

The year was ending today. The entire C&M office was soaked in celebration, everybody dressed snazzy, excited about the New Year waiting right at the door to enter. It was the end of the millennium; people had waited a hundred years for this. The clients also took a backseat that day for everyone waited for the annual feast to kick-start in the afternoon; an old C&M custom. A small stage was set up in the main hall, on which any employee could walk up and do what their heart desired; sing, dance, tell a story, their ambition, and expectations at C&M, say something nasty or heart-warming about their peers and seniors. It was all free that one day: food, liquor, and inhibition.

The New Year party started sharp at two. The music blared through the speakers placed across the hall, groups of young employees chatted animatedly, and a few jumped on the stage and danced. On one of the tables, some enthusiasts had already decided to compete on who could down the maximum tequila shots. They seemed to be in a rush to pass out soon. Krishna sat at his work station, looking at them making merry, caring a damn for the world, their lives so different than his.

It was late evening with revelry at its peak when their HR head went up on stage. She announced that the bar would be shut for an hour, lest everybody would collapse before midnight. It made sense to him, but not to most of the others for they booed loudly. She handled them with her charm and an oozing smile.

'It is time to unleash, it's time to break free,' she said and invited participation on stage. The crowd was apprehensive initially, only a few displaying enthusiasm, but soon the energy gathered momentum. A lot of them had come armed, with their guitars, flutes, mouthorgan and an odd one even carried the sitar. Everyone yearns to display and get appreciation for the potential they possess, but get limited opportunities, Krishna thought. Today they had the platform and a chance to perform in front of a large audience and no one wanted to miss it. All of them who came up on stage had a natural talent in what they did, be it a song they sang, dance, playing an instrument, telling a story or a joke, or even mouthing funny one liners about their bosses and friends. He couldn't do any of what others did there; except that he could perhaps tell a story. Even to do that, he would need to borrow one from her.

Shibani went up on stage to sing an English song; it seemed like a popular one as everyone sang along. She looked pretty in a black sleeveless dress that fell just a tad short above her knees. She held a glass of wine in her hand.

Rohit patted his shoulder. 'Aren't you doing something, mister?' he asked pointing towards the stage.

'I don't know any of it that they do.'

Shibani had finished and he saw her walking towards him. Without saying anything, she pulled his hand and made him stand up.

'It's your turn to go up.' She grinned.

'I can't. I know nothing,' he said. She didn't listen and pulled him up on the stage; Rohit eased her effort by pushing him from behind.

'Anything will do. It can even be a recently written copy,' she chuckled wickedly.

Krishna gazed at the C&M crowd, his heart pounding with anticipation. He had managed to take out his diary from the bag.

'Don't read the Sweet Beat ad,' she laughed standing next to the stage.

He remembered the last time he had spoken into the mike; it was for CSWI. Chhavi was with him, by his side.

He gave way to his words eventually, 'I don't know if you would like what I have written. Most of it is random. It's just how I am feeling in those moments.' The crowd seemed appreciative.

यह प्यार आखिर है क्या बला ?
इंतज़ार है तुम्हारे आने का या कि जाने की तकलीफ़

तुम्हारे हँसने से हुआ आनंद है या तुम्हारे रोने का दु:ख
तुम्हें छूने का अनूठा अहसास है या तुमसे दूर रहने का रहस्य
उस पहले चुम्बन की न भूली याद है या कि तुम्हारे अपमान पर
उबला मेरा गुस्सा
मेरे हाथों में गुथा तुम्हारा हाथ है या बारिश में बेपरवाह भीगता
तुम्हारा तन
मेरी कमीज़ के बटन में उलझा तुम्हारा लम्बा बाल है या तुम्हारी
आँख से लटका वह नमकीन आँसू
मेरे प्यार में सैकड़ो अनकहे शब्द हैं या तुम्हारी हर की गयी ज़िद से
मेरा हारना
तुम्हें वर्षों न मिल पाने का दु:ख है या तुम्हें पाने का निरंतर प्रयास
उस हर पल में दर्द से करवट बदलना है जिनमें न थी तुम, कि अब
जब अंत सामने है तो हंसना
चलो अब एक और मौका आया कि तुमसे एक बार फिर मिलूँ और
जानूँ
यह प्यार आखिर है क्या बला?

He ended, to look at the C&M office crowd. They looked stifled of expression, making him unsure about their liking. He could hear only one man clapping, the sound coming from the back of the hall. He gazed in that direction, a man with salt and pepper hair and a short beard, clapped briskly. Virag and a bunch of other senior people from the agency surrounded him. The crowd finally broke its stupor to cheer and clap heartily.

'That was a wonderful piece, Krishna. You can't walk away with just one of it,' the man shouted from behind. Krishna was a bit surprised that he knew his name. He had seen him walking in the corridor and with Virag sometimes.

इस सही को क्या मैं ढूँढूँ जब तक खुद गलत न करूँ
वह मंज़िल कहाँ से पाऊँ जब तक न भटकूँ
इस प्यार को मैं क्या समझूँ जब तक खुद न धोखा खाऊँ
तुम्हारी याद है क्या जानूँ जब तक अलग न हूँ
चेहरे पर क्या हँसी आये जो भरपेट न रो लूँ
आँखों में नींद क्यों छाये जो पसीने में लथपथ न हूँ
इस आस को क्या ही पालूँ जब तक न सब खो दूँ
तुम्हारा साथ क्यों है नाज़ुक क्या समझूँ जो तुमसे न बिछड़ूँ
तुम्हारा प्यार है कितना गहरा क्या जानूँ जो तुमसे न लड़ूँ
हर वादे का क्या है मोल जो इन्हें न तोड़ूँ
यह रौशनी कहाँ से पाऊँ जब तक अंधेरों में न भटकूँ
उस किनारे को कैसे खोजूँ जब तक खुद न गहरा डूबूँ
मैं अंत तक कैसे पहुँचूँ जब तक खुद न आरम्भ करूँ
यह मृत्यु कैसे मानूँ जब तक खुद न पूरा जी लूँ

Krishna saw the salt and pepper-haired man stand up and clap, giving him a standing ovation. Others sitting next to him followed. He was obviously a VIP in C&M.

Shibani looked at him intently. They were standing in a corner as she sipped from a glass of wine.

'I loved what you said Krishna...in each of the two pieces. The first that delves on the mystery of what love can really mean to different people. The second that harps on living life to its fullest. Not evaluating every step that you take, but just flow with it.'

He smiled. 'Thank You. I am glad that you liked it.'

Virag came in from behind. 'That rendition was fabulous. Look at me, the creative head who finds it so hard to write anything except for a client.'

'Maybe there is something Virag that you can do better than Krishna and all of us,' Shibani joked.

Virag gestured as if thinking hard, 'Cooking, maybe.' Everyone laughed.

'No, but truly it was real good. Even Super Boss was impressed,' he said.

'Who is that? The same gentleman you were standing with?' Krishna asked.

Virag nodded. 'Prashant Pandey. He is the Chairman and Managing Director of C&M.'

He entered his little modest quarter with Shibani close to midnight. The party was reaching its fag end, people fatigued with binging on alcohol. Shibani wanted to see where he lived and he had nothing to hide. She gazed around the room, probably overwhelmed with its space and how it could fit someone inside. He opened the window; the only thing that he could showoff was the view.

'It's a nice view from here,' she said gaping at the flyover. The cars zipped by, some of them with youngsters, stretching their hands out of the car windows holding beer bottles. The fireworks had started, expecting the New Year and a new millennium to break in any moment.

'It's my birthday tomorrow,' Krishna said, realizing suddenly.

'That's wonderful Krishna. Wish I knew this. I would have got you a present,' she slurred cupping his face.

He was stuck in her embrace. 'That's fine. The fireworks for the New Year reminded me or else I wouldn't have remembered at all.'

She stared at him. 'No. You need a present,' she said and kissed him on the lips. He could smell the strong perfume on her body and taste the residue of red wine over her tongue. He was stunned with her sudden burst of passion fuelled with alcohol running inside. She held his hands and placed them over her breasts. His hands quivered, feeling the chiffon on her body and skin that stiffened up with his touch.

'I am your birthday present. Accept me.' She smiled.

'No Shibani. Please don't do this.' He pulled himself back. She looked hurt for having her invitation turned down.

'Why? You don't like me?' she said looking frustrated with the dismissal.

'I love someone.'

Streaks of anger ran over her face. 'She is married and gone Krishna. By now, she would have probably forgotten you. Why don't you get it?'

'Maybe she has, but I still love her.'

'Then go and live in your fucking world. For all you know, she would be making love to her husband right now, as you refuse love here,' she screamed, her voice reeking of disbelief. She left his room, more hurt than angry.

The fireworks erupted in the skyline, signalling that another year had dawned. He stared at the flyover; people had stopped their vehicles on the road as they hugged each other, even strangers. He walked out of his room into the main hall. The building housekeeping had dimmed the lights after people had left. Some inebriated ones were strewn on the sofa languishing, hoping to gain senses again. He sat at his workstation and switched on the computer. He went to his e-mail account and typed his password krishnaandchhavi. The inbox indicated that there was a new message. He clicked on it, his heart thumping against his ribs, ready to pop out. Chhavi had written. *Happy Birthday Krishna.*

He read it many times over, before he cried, vindicated about his trust in her.

Prashant Pandey called him to his office the next afternoon. He entered it hesitatingly, admiring its plush interiors, not knowing that C&M nestled such a beauty inside. Prashant chatted with Virag, who listened with rapt attention. Prashant noticed his presence and gestured at the vacant chair. They spoke about some studio, called Crescent, which was into making films. He wondered why he had been called there.

'So, how have you been Krishna? Do you like it here at C&M?' Prashant asked, resting his head on the cushioned chair.

'Yes sir. I like it here,' he said.

'Haven't you briefed him about the C&M culture?' Prashant looked at Virag.

'I have Prashant. He is overwhelmed, meeting the Chairman on the first day of the year.' Virag grinned as he glanced at Krishna. 'The same rule applies in this office as well. Not to address anyone as Sir.' Krishna nodded.

Prashant leaned forward. 'You write very well from what I heard last evening. What else have you written?'

'Mostly poetry and some experiences that I don't want to part with.'

'Can I see some of it?' Prashant asked.

He got his diary from the work station and handed it over.

'It's all over the pages, written haphazardly, it would be difficult for you to figure out.'

'I will manage.' Prashant smiled as he flipped through the pages. They finished coffee and waited for his attention.

Prashant kept his diary on the table and gazed at him. 'Most of it is very good. I think he can do the job,' he said and looked at Virag.

'Thank you,' Krishna replied.

'I am making a film,' he paused, 'besides pursuing clients for C&M of course. To do the latter I have many people to help, like him,' he pointed at Virag. Virag smirked. 'But to do the former, hardly any,' he said.

Krishna looked at him blankly, not knowing what Prashant wanted from him.

He got up to stand near the large window that ran between the two ends of the wall. 'Ever since I started C&M, I have wanted to make films, perhaps direct one. But never got a chance until now. I went to the studio with a story that I had in mind and they loved the outline of it. All of them are my friends, we meet socially, have a drink together at a party. But when it comes to funding the movie, you have to get down to brass tracks. You need a hard-bound script along with the business math.'

He took a sip of water. 'I can do the math, but I can't trust my story with people I don't know. It's tough you know, giving your child to someone else, expecting that they take care of it the way you would. It's tough.' Prashant nodded, thinking.

He sat on his chair again and leaned on the table. 'I am making a film for the first time and for that I need people whom I can trust. Will you help us in making this story better?' he looked into Krishna's eyes.

His coming to the point straightway was too sudden. Krishna had never expected it. His deep buried fear raised its ugly head again.

He scurried through his words. 'I am not experienced enough to do this. I won't be able to do justice to your story.'

Prashant looked at Virag, gesturing at him to intervene.

'You won't be working on it alone, so don't hassle yourself. It will be a small team, Prashant himself, you and I,' Virag said calmly.

Krishna thought of Chhavi, the destination she wanted him to reach, the path he had to walk through. Was this a conspiracy that she had laid out with the universe to show him the way? Wasn't this an opportunity that had fallen in his lap, just by itself, waiting to be picked up? Then where was the hitch coming from? He had to let it go.

'Okay, I will do this. I may need a lot of help though,' Krishna said.

'We are in it together from now. We are collaborating together and no help. Okay?' Prashant winked. He took out a folder from his drawer and handed it to Krishna.

'I have spent half of my life in small towns before I met up with this monster of a city. This story has a lot about the spirit of these towns,' he said.

Krishna looked away through the window, at the reflection of the sun on the façade of the building opposite to theirs. 'I have stayed there as well.'

Prashant nodded. 'Virag has briefed me about it. With your gifted craft and familiarity with the language, I think you will do a great job.' He glanced at Virag. 'We need a solid story, from the detailed outline that I have written. After we finish that, I will give it to Ranjit to write the screenplay with his writers. Then we go to Crescent. Ok?'

'So when do we get to see the first draft Krishna?' he asked. Krishna flipped through the pages; there were 120 odd A4 sheets. He had never done this job before; he had no idea.

'It took me about a month to write this from scratch. Now that you have it,' he pointed towards his folder, 'it shouldn't take you more than two weeks to make it better.'

'What's the difference between a story and a screenplay?' Krishna asked Virag after coming out of Prashant's office.

Virag smiled at his unabashed naivety. 'Well, a story is one that you read in a book. A screenplay approaches that story in a very different manner structurally, representing each instance of the story in its minutest details; the text version of a moving picture, frame by frame.'

Krishna nodded.

'You just focus on bettering his story. Prashant is very well connected with everyone in the entertainment industry. If Crescent has liked his story, he will be able to sell it. We can ride the tide with him, if we stick to what he wants us to deliver.'

'Krishna, I am really sorry,' Shibani said sitting on the empty chair next to his work station.

'That's fine. You were messed up with both, head as well as heart,' he preferred gazing at the computer screen than her, embarrassed.

'I was drunk and over last few days I had developed feelings for you,' she said candidly staring at the carpet. It was hard to imagine a full on aggressive girl like Shibani behave like this. Circumstances do have the ability to overpower people and force them to do stupid things.

'I made some nasty comments that would have hurt you badly. No?' She looked up.

'I have been used to such comments all my life. Moreover, if it was not for you and Virag, I wouldn't have survived at C&M.'

'You are being modest. You ooze talent.'

'I am serious.'

'Will you pardon me for my stupidity?'

Krishna smiled at Shibani. It was hard to find people with such transparent souls; for if some day they could smother you with their harshness, the next day they could win you over with their unpretentious heart.

Life can be both, unfair and fair, all of a sudden. What seemed completely unfair to him a few months back when his life changed its course and landed him in Mumbai, looked better today. In a matter of two days, he was starting work on a film, it seemed unreal.

He completed reading Prashant's draft at midnight and kept it aside. It was a good story, emotional and very gripping. Three women living in different parts of the world and leading different lives, receive a letter each. All the three letters are from one man; the three of them have known him and shared a relationship with him at some point in their life. One knew him at school, another in college and the third when she worked at a radio station.

He calls all of them on one particular day in Mussoorie to return something that he has. The draft was divided into three parts, one for each of the three love stories and then the climax. He loved Prashant's detailing and nuances about the small towns across the first two love stories: the first set in Agra, and the second in Jaipur. There were certain things in it where he itched to elaborate and also make some changes. The second love story set in Jaipur looked similar to the first one; it needed spice. The first he thought could be expanded a bit. The third looked just fine, but for the climax. He didn't agree with what Prashant had written; it was what one would expect and warm your heart. He didn't want the story to end how routine love stories usually do. The hero gets the girl he loves the most, after a lot of heartburn, endless chase and just before everyone would think it's all over. Voila! They unite, never to separate again. He wanted to write the climax, his way.

Krishna gave his all over the next two weeks. He juggled sleeplessly between the C&M responsibility and Prashant's story, so much so that he lost track of time. Shibani had started calling him a walking zombie. It was as if his life depended on that one chance that destiny had granted to him miraculously. This assignment became his reason to exist, the story he embraced into his being; Virag and he would have endless arguments to agree on something, after which Krishna would rewrite. He finished the story a few hours before the fifteenth day dawned, and emailed it to Prashant.

Prashant came to the office during late second half and called them into his room. Krishna entered the room with Virag, apprehension looming large over his heart. Prashant was flipping through a docket, Krishna could make out that it was a printout of the revised story. He kept it on the table and looked at them. His expression softened; they suddenly felt comforted.

Prashant walked to the bar in one corner of the room and grabbed a bottle of scotch, 'Drink?'

'I don't mind,' Virag said. Prashant looked at Krishna, who nodded.

He handed them the glasses and took a sip. 'I read the revised story, complete. You have made quite a few changes to it. It reads well.' He nodded, thinking.

Krishna squirmed in his seat. 'We have taken a few liberties, Prashant. I am sorry if that's disturbing you. We can always revert to the original.'

'No, that's all right. Just fine,' he said, picking up the docket, some pages in it marked with red post-it. He turned over the first marked page.

'You have changed the ending of first part; I had written that the boy and his first love in school separate at the school gate. It was meant to be symbolic, teenage love ending at the school gate. You changed the location to a railway platform?' he looked at Krishna questioningly.

'It was his first love,' Krishna spoke slowly, 'and the deepest. I thought the earlier end was a bit casual, the platform sequence adds the pain of separation and sticks to your memory better.'

Prashant nodded. 'It's very moving though.' He went to another marked page.

'In the second part, you have changed the setting of the story from Jaipur to Lucknow, though most of the episodes are retained as they were.'

Krishna cleared his throat. 'I have added student politics as the backdrop to the second love story. There are a few chapters that highlight the political bickering happening in university corridors. Frankly, I had no idea of how I could write about student politics, if Jaipur was the city.'

Virag intervened, 'Krishna has seen student politics from close quarters in Lucknow. We had discussed this in detail before changing it. It doesn't take away anything from the second part, Prashant. The love story is left as it was, except for changing the setting and locations that he knew about,' he said glancing at Krishna.

'No, I agree. It's reading tighter, racy, and compact,' Prashant shrugged. 'Though I would like to make some corrections to it.'

'But of course boss,' Virag said.

'You guys haven't done much in the third part though, except for developing some chapters more extensively and adding a couple of characters more,' he said.

Krishna took the last sip from his glass. 'There wasn't much to do in the third part. It was written very well. Just that some chapters needed detailing.'

Prashant poured himself another scotch.

'Where's the climax? You haven't included that in your draft. Do you think the one that I have written is good to go?' Prashant gazed at them.

Virag glanced at Krishna. 'Yeah, we had a discussion over it. Krishna wasn't too happy.'

'Do you want to make some amends to it?' Prashant asked.

Krishna was keyed up, oscillating between speaking up and holding within.

'I don't like the climax in it its current form. It's weakening the story,' he said.

Prashant raised his eyebrow. 'Don't like it? What do you mean?'

'The protagonist sacrifices his love each time for all the three girls and in the end chooses one out of them to live happily ever after. This is weakening the intensity of the story; this won't move people.'

'How can you say this?' Prashant took another gulp of scotch, a bit agitated. 'Happy endings are all about hope that people today are losing. It makes one believe that they too have a chance, despite of all the challenges that they grapple with.'

'Boss, you are right. But this story can't have an end like this. All the three love stories end in separation. He never gets love when he wants it the most. He finding love in one out of the three would raise a question mark on the remaining two,' Krishna said.

'But one of them is married and the other girl is a divorcee. He finds love in the third girl,' Prashant said hastily.

Krishna was getting wearier by the minute. 'That's what my point is. You can't choose a girl in the end, who used you for your own selfish means, over the other two women,' he paused. 'We have built the protagonist's character all along in the story. The end would make him look so fragile, contrary to what he is.'

Prashant had started shaking his head before Krishna finished. 'I have given birth to this story Krishna. I know how it will grow and end. Sorry, but I won't like to tinker with the climax.'

Krishna attempted to protest, one last time, but Virag intervened.

'It's your story boss. You will decide how it will end. Let's leave it at that,' he said. Krishna kept silent, his demeanour not in agreement with theirs.

Prashant had calmed down by then. 'Nevertheless, my hunch was right. You guys have turned it better. In fact, much better than what it was. I will work on it now to refine it a bit more and then we fix up with Crescent.' He smiled. Both Krishna and Virag hi-fived and let out a cheer.

Just before leaving his office, Krishna pulled out some sheets from his bag and handed it to Prashant.

'Boss, here is another version of the climax that I had written. You have all the right to put it in the garbage bin, but before you do that, please read it once. This is my humble request. '

Krishna faintly heard the sound of the banging on his door before the noise became more distinct. He had been numbed by sleep that he had been pushing aside for over two weeks. He opened the door; it was the day guard from the reception. He informed Krishna that Prashant Pandey was on the phone. It was seven in the morning and this surprised him.

'Did I wake you up Krishna?' Prashant sounded tentative.

'Good Morning Prashant. Yes, I was fast asleep.'

'I didn't know that you live in one of the rooms in office. Virag told me just now.'

'Virag helped me; it's very convenient.'

Prashant cleared his throat. 'Krishna, can you come home?'

He was surprised. 'Now?'

'Yes. I am sending the car.'

An hour later, Krishna was sitting in Prashant's upscale luxurious apartment in Worli, overlooking the sea.

Prashant entered the room wearing track pants and a t-shirt. He looked unslept and sported dark circles under his eyes. Krishna got up from the cushioned sofa; Prashant gestured at him to relax. He sat opposite him.

'You would be wondering why I called you all of a sudden.'

'There would be a reason, boss.'

Prashant nodded, thinking.

'I gave the draft that you guys had written to my wife. She is my fiercest critic and it's her opinion I respect the most,' he paused. 'She read through it, way past midnight.'

'What did she say?'' Krishna asked.

'She was emotionally overwhelmed and couldn't sleep for a long time. But what moved her most was the climax.'

'I am very pleased to hear this, Prashant.' Krishna smiled.

Prashant was staring at him, 'She read the climax you wrote, and not the earlier one. She had read the last one before.'

His words pierced Krishna's heart like sharp arrows and unleashed serendipity.

'Did you read it too?' Krishna mumbled.

Prashant got up and walked up to him. 'Yes, I gave it to her after having gone through it. The end is brilliant. It takes the story to another level.'

Krishna got up to clasp his hand, his eyes brimming with tears. 'Your words mean a lot to me. I can't thank you enough for giving me this opportunity.'

'God has gifted each one of us with a unique potential,' Prashant paused. 'That one thing which only we can do, better than most of the others. Some of us spend our entire lives unaware about our hidden potential, while others despite knowing of it do nothing about it. So it goes waste.'

He wrapped his arm around Krishna's shoulder. 'You are lucky for discovering it so early in life. Keep polishing it, for it has the power to light up millions of lives besides yours.'

Krishna nodded slowly. Memories of Chhavi, her belief in him, his writing, caressed his being lovingly; and then soaked him in.

few months had passed since then. Krishna was back in his old job as the C&M copy writer, his stature though graduated rapidly. There was hardly any important pitch that C&M participated in and didn't involve him. Clients had discovered him, his existence in the large agency, referring to his opinion in all their key marketing campaigns. He was promoted as senior copy writer with a substantial hike in his salary. He started saving more for his family, and sent more money back home to Jalegar. Prashant Pandey had been successful in cracking his film deal with Crescent. He couldn't rest at one place in his office after meeting them; the passion cooped inside had finally found a vent. The studio had loved the story, he said, and was ready to put in more money than he had expected. The studio wanted to know which film stars he had in mind. Prashant had done all his homework; C&M had created the advertising blitz for launching Saahil, the son of yester-year actor and now a director, Rakesh Kohli. Rakesh was going through rough times, his last two films doing badly at the box office. Saahil was his last bet but he was left with little money to create an impact and showcase his son to the world. Prashant had helped out Rakesh by not charging a penny for the advertising campaign that C&M created for his son.

C&M launched Saahil with a unique identity, the lover boy who could dance better than anyone else in the film industry. It worked! The movie was a super hit and Saahil became an overnight sensation. Prashant knew it was time for Rakesh Kohli to return the favour. He asked Rakesh Kohli to let his son play the lead in his debut film – *Love Hamesha* (Love Always). Rakesh Kohli liked his script, but more than it, he couldn't overlook Prashant's support, when he had needed it the most.

The story of *Love Hamesha* centered on the main protagonist who had in lead, Saahil Kohli the hottest emerging star of the film industry. Getting rest of the cast was no big deal. Crescent was elated with Prashant's farsightedness for he had plugged the biggest gap beforehand. Prashant Pandey threw a lavish bash at his residence to announce his new plunge. Virag and Krishna were invited to the party where Prashant introduced him as the writer to watch out for, to everyone. People were curious to know more about him, none wanting to stamp him down or question his existence in a place that was far beyond his reach. That whole evening when people made merry, he wished if she could have been there with him...maybe just for a few moments. Unlike other memories that seem to fade away with the passage of time, hers grew sharper with each passing day. His heart, squeezing them tightly, was refusing to let even a bit of her reminiscence escape. Prashant gave him a new name that day, KK. He said Krishna Kumar was too boring, now that he was a part of the entertainment world. He had an email id by that name; she had created it months back. Soon, the name given to him by his parents faded away into oblivion and he was known as KK to all.

Prashant Pandey called Virag and him to the airport while leaving for location hunting along with his crew. They were travelling to Agra, Lucknow and then to Delhi. He wanted Krishna to come with him to Lucknow for his know-how, about all the places that he had written about in *Love Hamesha*. Krishna had declined politely, saying that he was required more at C&M than in tracking those places in Lucknow. He had lied; for having gone there and not meeting her would further torture his wounds that he had been able to nurse till then, somehow. Prashant had not pressed him beyond a point. Prashant had also told him then, that he would be sharing the story credit in *Love Hamesha* with Krishna. It delighted him even more when Prashant agreed to include Virag's name in it as well, on his persistence. The shooting of *Love Hamesha* was wrapped up quickly as Saahil Kohli had other films waiting, where he was being paid much more. *Love Hamesha* went into post production and as it neared release, Prashant launched the weaponry that he was most familiar with – a marketing juggernaut.

C&M worked fulltime as a unit on *Love Hamesha,* as if it was their own film. Krishna worked his heart out along with the C&M team for he wanted his first tryst of commercial writing to work by any means. Having held hands with failure so many times in his life, this was one such time when he had to succeed for himself, his family, for so many others like him in his village and... for her. If she knew what he was going through at that time, she would be praying for him. He was sure about that.

Love Hamesha was scheduled to release around Christmas that year. Prashant had told him that this was the most favourable time for any film to release, besides Diwali. People are in a holiday mode as both Christmas and New Year are clubbed together and if the film is good, it can do roaring business. Krishna didn't understand this kind of math much; for all that he was interested in films, was writing.

The entire C&M team had been called for a special screening of *Love Hamesha* at Liberty Theatre in Marine Lines. Krishna had accompanied Virag in his car and during their travel, they glanced at quite a few large billboards of their film. Virag had stopped his car excitedly under one of them, as they gazed at Sahil Kohli striking a pose with the three heroines in the movie. They would have seen that creative over a million times on the computer, but seeing it live on that road and being noticed by millions of others was another high.

Saahil Kohli couldn't attend the special screening as he was shooting in London for his next spy thriller. The three heroines turned up looking gorgeous; the entire C&M team was very excited to see them as they shook their hands and took autographs. Prashant got him and Virag to meet with them, introducing them as the co-writers on *Love Hamesha*. The ladies praised the story no end, commenting that it was a first for them, when a film had tested their acting skills. Krishna would discover in the years to come that actors had this habit to admire all their films like this. The Crescent Studio team came dressed in their stiff suits. Prashant sat with them in the first row, knowing well where the money purse rested.

Love Hamesha started rolling on the wide white screen. It had been a few months before Krishna had seen his last movie, the one that starred Saahil Kohli, for he wanted to see who was reprising the role that he had helped write. The credits appeared to fade out from the screen as he sat with his eyes fixated. Shibani cheered and kissed him on the cheek as the story credits appeared. It said Prashant Pandey, KK, and Virag Joshi. KK looked so small, suspended between the two heavy-weight names. Prashant hadn't told him this. If he had, perhaps he would have resisted. He glanced at Shibani looking at the screen with rapt attention and felt glad about how their relationship had evolved over the last one year. She was now his best friend in the city.

The special screening of *Love Hamesha* didn't have an interval, so when it ended, it was greeted with a standing ovation. The C&M staff kept clapping till Prashant intervened and gestured at everyone to stop. Krishna was blown away by the sheer experience of watching words unfold themselves into life, on the giant screen in flesh and blood. He thought that Prashant had done a commendable job by giving life to the sincere story that they had jointly created. As a debutant filmmaker, it was certain that Prashant had charted out his course in the film industry. Prashant hugged Virag and him as they cut a huge cake along with the film's heroines. The C&M crowd kept cheering for a long time. Prashant invited the two of them to the film's premiere the next day, where the entire cast and crew of *Love Hamesha*, and some prominent people from the film and media industry would be present. He said this was just the beginning; the real test would begin once the movie opened in theatres a day later.

The New Year had arrived hurriedly. The customary office party had got over early. Prashant was not in town, travelling across the country, checking out the public and trade response to *Love Hamesha*. Krishna had been anxious since the time he had left the screening, waiting to hear if someone living in Delhi or Lucknow and in his village Jalegar liked it as much as him. He wondered if Chhavi knew that he was a part of creating this film, had Virag told her. If she did, then whether she had watched it, with her friends or husband or someone else. Did the film remind her of him just like he remembered her every moment while writing that story?

Shibani had asked Krishna to wait as she went back to Bandra to pick up her fiancé Tarun. She wanted to spend the New Year with only the two of them. It was twelve and the fireworks had erupted to light up the Mumbai skyline. There was a beep on his recently-purchased mobile phone. It was Prashant.

'KK! My man,' Prashant sounded on top of the world.

'*Love Hamesha* has nailed it,' he said. Suddenly Krishna felt the unbearable weight on his chest lighten. The noise of fireworks at both ends drowning their voices.

'Where are you calling from Prashant?'

'Lucknow, at this theatre called Novelty. Despite it being the New Year's Eve, the theatre is packed. The film is a runaway hit. The distributors, exhibitors and Crescent... everyone is so bloody happy.'

'Lucknow?' Krishna felt an uncanny happiness surging inside on hearing it.

'Yes. Tomorrow I am in Delhi, hopping across a few theatres before I hit Mumbai,' Prashant almost shouted into his mobile phone.

'And KK, you know what?'

'What Boss?'

'People are shedding tears by the buckets. The climax has worked. It has worked big time.'

'KK?' Prashant said not hearing a word from Krishna.

'Yes boss.'

'I think we guys have arrived in this industry. Cheers and Happy New Year. We will party the day after,' he said.

'Sure, boss.'

Krishna reached for the desktop on his workstation and typed the e-mail account and his password hurriedly. The message for which he had waited the entire year had arrived. *Happy Birthday Krishna.*

He came down from the C&M building on the road and walked with rapid steps. The streets of the city were flooded with vehicles and people on the pavements, both trying to avoid bumping into each other. Krishna scuttled his way through them, walking briskly at first and then breaking into a run. His life ran in his mind like a film, in patches. The painful memories from his past appearing like sharp piercing lances as he ran through them, facing their hit relentlessly. He picked up his speed to run faster as the lances increased in numbers. He was breathless but undefeated when he reached Haji Ali. The Haji Ali Dargah looked radiant, submerged in the sea. He looked sideways, a *Love Hamesha* billboard perched regally on the Haji Ali circle.

The emotion overwhelmed his breathlessness soon, as he wept sitting on the ledge, uncontrollably.

KK was born that night.

Lucknow: 2nd January, 2016

Ram Singh's face looked anguished. It was visible in the early morning sunlight that seeped in from the sky. The Mercedes speeded freely now, after having met with some congestion on the Ganga Bridge in Kanpur. Lucknow was at hand.

'I can now understand your sense of urgency in wanting to see madam,' Ram Singh muttered. 'She is the only lifeline that you have. Any risk to it would hurt your life as well.'

'Yes,' KK said.

Ram Singh pulled over outside the bungalow. The bungalow looked barren. It was early in the morning; the large entrance gates were unmanned, contrary to what they looked years before – a stream of security guards lining up the pathway starting from the main gates. Today KK walked inside the brooding house alone, gazing at its pale walls, which had lost its sheen to the years of neglect. His heart pounded with every measured step that he took, not knowing what lay unfolded ahead. He rang the door-bell and waited. The door creaked and a lanky, old, house help emerged. KK asked if Chhavi was there. The man looked a tad surprised as if KK was at the wrong address. Then he asked him to sit, as he disappeared into the house. KK gazed inside; everything looked the same since the last time that he had met Panditji there, till he turned around to see the wall behind. A huge portrait of Pandit Radhey Shankar Mishra hung on the wall, garlanded. He sat down on the cushioned sofa, saddened with this sudden realization. The pain that he felt then, strangely matched the intensity of the moment, when he lit his father's funeral pyre in the village seven years ago. The house help interrupted his thought and handed him an envelope that was marked to him. KK gestured at him if he could read it there. The servant nodded. He read her letter that she had left for him:

Krishna

I know there would come a day when you would reach my door and get this letter that I am leaving with my grandmother. She is the only one who knows everything about us; she is my confidante, my mother, and the keeper of all my secrets. By the time you read this letter, I would have been gone for months. Grandmother is old now, so it was tough for me to leave her alone, but staying here any more is tougher. This city has turned me into a pauper.

Every year that I have lived after you left has made me lose something. After letting you go, it was Baba's choice to leave me. I have by now lived half my life with people who I don't love. The marriage between me and Sudhanshu was never appropriate. I could share my bed with him, but never my heart. He was careless with his drink and that cost him his life in an accident last year. I didn't grieve his death, for my heart could never beat for him. My brothers got busy with their own lives and separated along with their families after Baba died. I can't complain about them, for they have families to take care of. I have none except my old grandmother. Sudhanshu was eager to start a family, a thought I detested. Out of the three obligations that a woman is supposed to meet in her life that Baba mentioned, I have fulfilled two, that of a daughter and then a wife. I wasn't ready to take care of the third; mothering the child of someone I didn't love. It would have been a sin. So I kept resisting till the day death took Sudhanshu away.

After we parted that day on the railway station, I had locked you in the biggest room, inside my heart, and threw the keys away in the Gomti River. Your memories grew fonder by the days that passed and when I lost Baba, there wasn't a reason for me to smile. My loneliness was turning me senile when I decided that it was better to run away, leaving behind my bag of memories. Better than dying under its weight. Sudhanshu's absence gave me the courage to take this step.

There is a thread that binds us together and even if we don't see or feel it, it wouldn't cease to exist. I have pulled it today, Krishna. If it tugs you as strongly, come back, or else return to your future that dazzles. I can spend all my life remembering you within every moment that I live.

Chhavi

Krishna put her letter inside his shirt pocket. He asked the house help where her grandmother was. The servant led him inside.

Her grandmother was wrapped in a thick quilt; it was January for the northern part of the country. Only the creases over her forehead twitched as the old woman saw him sit next to her.

'Krishna?' her voice trembled. He nodded, acknowledging his presence.

She handed him a piece of paper that had an address.

'Will you go?' her voice quivered.

'Yes. Right now, Nani,' he said.

KK sat in the car carrying an envelope in his hand. Ram Singh looked at him and turned on the ignition.

'Were you able to meet madam?'

KK shook his head, thinking. He took a deep breath.

'This story has to end today.'

'Which story sahib?'

'Our story, Ram Singh,' KK said.

'We need to drive to Pangot. It's near Nainital. Do you know the way?'

Ram Singh shook his head looking ahead.

'Is Chhavi madam there?' Ram Singh asked tentatively.

'Yes.'

'Then we will find the way, sahib.'

It took them a while to pass through the bustle of Nainital before the road became narrower. Their path meandered through a steep hill on one side and on the other there lay a deep valley. The weather in the hills had played truant and it had suddenly turned chilly. KK had planned for winters in the north and was carrying warm clothes. They reached Pangot, and it was four in the evening when KK checked his watch.

They kept asking for directions till their car faced the gates of a cottage. The name plate said – "Chhavi Shankar Mishra". KK got off the car and asked Ram Singh to wait there. The cottage rested on the slope of a hill and he could spot birds of different varieties perched on its roof. He took a deep breath and filled his lungs with the clean fresh air of the hills. It was a large cottage, diffused light emanating from its windows, and a striking garden on one side. It was as if one were looking at a painting. KK saw her sitting there, at the edge of the garden facing the hill. She sat on a wooden bench under a shade designed to savour breathtaking views that hills offer. KK walked towards her. She was deep in thought, sucked into her world. He sat next to her and clasped her hand. Chhavi didn't shudder as if she was expecting this touch. She then smiled looking at him as if she had redeemed all of those sixteen years in that one moment; that they had lost together.

'So, you came.'

'I had promised. You had to pull the thread once. It took you long.'

'What if I had not?'

'I would have waited.'

'Why?'

'Can I tell you a story?'

'So you have a grandmother as well?' She smiled.

'I can write my own stories now.'

She nodded.

In a kingdom there lived a very poor man who made excellent flutes. Though he was an expert at making them, he could sell very few and thus could hardly make his ends meet. He fell in love with a beautiful girl belonging to an extremely rich family. She would often advise him to expand his business of making flutes, but he would always be reluctant saying that there was no future in this business. He would complain all day of how insignificant his talent of making flutes was and that God had cheated him by not granting him any special skills. One day the girl invited the man over to her house. She treated him with an array of tasty dishes and the best of wine. The poor man had never experienced such a feast so he ate a lot and drank as much wine as he could. After a while he got drunk and then soon passed out. The girl took out a very precious jewel from her vault and stitched it discreetly in the man's robe.

The next day when the man gained consciousness he found himself lying in his old dilapidated hut. He went out to look for the girl, only to discover that she had vanished. Their house was empty too. The man sunk into despair of having been cheated by her. He cursed the girl repeatedly. Soon he decided to leave the city and settle elsewhere. While he was walking to the nearby kingdom, his robe got torn a bit. He went to a tailor in the new kingdom, who while stitching the robe discovered the precious jewel. The man was overjoyed but didn't know who had put it there. He brushed that thought aside and sold off the jewel. It fetched him lot of money with which he built a nice house and started living a life of luxury. He couldn't forget the girl, so he hired a messenger and sent him to the old kingdom to find out if she had come back. The girl had not returned. He started living off his wealth again, but soon it started diminishing with the passage of time. The man was worried and his old days of poverty haunted him. He decided to do something *to earn money. He put his money in lot of businesses, but all of them failed. He was almost bankrupt now. He was left with only one option – of making flutes. For it was the only thing he knew. He thought about the girl he loved and how she had always said that no one could make a better flute than him.*

He started making flutes and selling them in the local market. Soon his business grew a little. He hired the messenger again and sent him to look for the missing girl. He came back empty handed. One day the king was passing through the market and he heard the sound of the flute that the man was playing in his shop. The king loved the music and the melodious haunting melody of the flute touched his heart. He summoned the man and ordered him to make a special flute for him. The man agreed and obeyed his orders. The king was so pleased with the flute, that he paid him a price. An amount that the man couldn't even dream of. Meanwhile, the man sent the messenger once again looking for the girl. This time too, the result was the same. The king became a patron of the man's flute. Seeing their emperor buying his flutes from the man, everyone in the kingdom started following the king. Shortly, he became one of the wealthiest and most cherished citizens of the kingdom. It had been a while that the man had visited his old kingdom. So he set off on the journey himself. To his utter surprise and delight, the girl he loved had returned and welcomed him. The years had taken away his anger and what remained was pure love.

He asked her, 'Why did you go?'

She smiled and said, 'If I didn't, you wouldn't have changed.'

The man thought about it for a while. 'Why didn't you come back earlier?'

She replied, 'I wanted to, but that would have meant that you would have returned to be with me, leaving everything.'

The man was confused. 'So?'

She explained, 'You would never have realized that your true potential lay in making flutes. I loved you and waited till the time you discovered it fully.'

KK finished and inched closer to her, wrapping his arm around her shoulders.

'You came into my life and changed my destiny, Chhavi. I would have waited even if it was for a lifetime.'

Her eyes moistened, 'Time has ripened your writing skills Krishna. I have seen all your films.'

KK smiled. 'You think I wouldn't know that?'

They laughed together.

'How did you reach here?' she asked.

'We drove down from Mumbai. It took us about forty hours.'

'You should take some rest then. And when do you have to return?'

'Never. I am not leaving now.'

She couldn't hide her happiness anymore. It resurfaced passionately after having deluded her life for long.

'Are you serious?'

'More than ever,' he said.

They sat quietly for over an hour, gazing at the hill. 'Krishna, have you ever been to Paris?' she asked childlike.

'Yes, a few times.'

'Will you take me there? It's a city I am longing to see.'
He nodded, smiling.

Ram Singh Yadav was ready to leave Pangot after having spent a couple of days.

'Have a safe trip Ram Singh and do give us a call when you reach,' she said handing him a packed lunch box and an envelope with cash. Ram Singh was hesitant but Chhavi persisted till he accepted. KK was talking on the phone with his secretary Gokhale. He gestured at Ram Singh to wait.

He finished the call and walked with him to the parked car.

'Sahib, when will you be coming to Mumbai next?'

'If Mumbai needs me, it will call me, or else I am just fine here.' KK smiled.

Ram Singh nodded. 'I was privileged to be by your side in your journey to find Chhavi madam.'

'What about your house and office, sahib?'

'Gokhale will take care of all that, Ram Singh.'

'And meetings?' Ram Singh asked with concern.

'I can always fly down if my presence is required. Otherwise we are all connected in today's time,' KK said raising his mobile phone.

'Moreover, Chhavi doesn't want to move to Mumbai right now.'

'Sahib, I can feel the love she carries for you in her heart. You are taking the right decision in choosing it over everything else. I wish I could get such a chance once,' he said reminiscing.

KK hugged him. 'You have a pure soul, Ram Singh. In the end, your happiness will always outstrip the pain.'

It was a full moon night. The moon was up casting its pale white reflection on the pond. She rested her head on his chest, looking at the iPad; she was crouched between his legs. They had left for Paris after staying in Pangot for a couple of months. After coming back, she wanted to visit Jalegar. Krishna had changed the way his people lived in his village, helping them to build stable and more reliable houses. He helped as many as he could. His house had also grown bigger and turned better. The number of buffaloes had grown too; there were six of them now. After his father passed away, his mother was left alone. Earlier, she would refuse to stay with him, but this time she had relented and accepted Chhavi's proposal to stay with them. She was packing her bags; they would leave an aide back to take care of the crop that grew on their land, and the buffaloes. Krishna had fulfilled his father's wish of owning a piece of land in Jalegar. Ganesh, his brother, had a good mind and he pursued higher education. Now he worked as a senior executive in a multinational bank in Delhi.

Chhavi flipped through the pictures and her memories of Paris. Krishna and her holding hands, standing in front of the magically illuminated Eiffel Tower; she, lazing on the chair under the red awning of Café Montparnasse; she, trying out a dress at the grand Louis Vuitton store at Champs

Elysees – a picture that he took discreetly for it showed a lot of her cleavage; him gazing at the Eiffel Tower, at the Seine River cruise. The last picture of him was her favourite.

'I wish we had gadgets like these when we were in the University,' she said.

'Why?' He stroked her hair.

'We would at least be having some pictures with us that we could look at, when we were estranged,' she said.

'Oh Yes! Absolutely,' Krishna nodded, his chin touching her hair. 'I would have also known how much you have aged since then.'

'What do you mean? Are you saying that I am old?' she turned around, acting angry. 'Look at you, graying on the sides.'

'Men are like wine darling, they get better with age. That's what women say,' he tickled her once in the stomach. She quivered.

'Why did you marry an old woman? Tell me,' she persisted with her angry teasing.

'This old man didn't have a better option,' he said and tickled her again repeatedly. She pushed him back on the mattress, laughing with him till they were rolling on the cot.

And then, Chhavi and Krishna made love.